Family Business

The Atonement

Book V

Family Business Series

Family Business V

The Atonement

Vanessa

Miller

Book V

Family Business Series

Printed in the United States of America

© 2018 by Vanessa Miller

Praise Unlimited Enterprises

Charlotte, NC

Other Books by Vanessa Miller

Family Business Book I

Family Business II - Sword of Division

Family Business III - Love and Honor

Family Business IV - The Children

Family Business V - The Atonement

Sunshine and Rain

Rain in the Promised Land

After the Rain

How Sweet the Sound

Heirs of Rebellion

Heaven Sent

Feels Like Heaven

Heaven on Earth

The Best of All

Better for Us

Her Good Thing

Long Time Coming

A Promise of Forever Love

A Love for Tomorrow

Yesterday's Promise

Forgotten

Forgiven

Forsaken

Rain for Christmas (Novella)

Through the Storm

Rain Storm

Latter Rain

Abundant Rain

Former Rain

Anthologies (Editor)

Keeping the Faith

Have A Little Faith

This Far by Faith

EBOOKS

Love Isn't Enough

A Mighty Love

The Blessed One (Blessed and Highly Favored series)

The Wild One (Blessed and Highly Favored Series)

The Preacher's Choice (Blessed and Highly Favored Series)

The Politician's Wife (Blessed and Highly Favored Series)

The Playboy's Redemption (Blessed and Highly Favored Series)

Tears Fall at Night (Praise Him Anyhow Series)

Joy Comes in the Morning (Praise Him Anyhow Series)

A Forever Kind of Love (Praise Him Anyhow Series)

Ramsey's Praise (Praise Him Anyhow Series)

Escape to Love (Praise Him Anyhow Series)

Praise for Christmas (Praise Him Anyhow Series)

His Love Walk (Praise Him Anyhow Series)

Could This Be Love (Praise Him Anyhow Series)

Song of Praise (Praise Him Anyhow Series)

Prologue

Obadiah Damerae Shepherd was conflicted. On one hand, this was supposed to be the happiest day of his life. He was graduating from one of the most prestigious Christian colleges in the US, and he had already secured a position as a youth pastor for a church in North Carolina. Still, something gnawed at him. Dam had this feeling of great dread as if something was about to happen that would change him in some profound way.

God had not revealed to him whether this change would be for the good or bad, so Dam was very cautious as he went through the motions of dressing for his big day. Everything from putting on his shoes to knotting his tie was done in slow motion as if he was standing in a cloud of fog that he couldn't cut through.

Then came the knock on his dorm room door. It was time, he was about to graduate and then become youth pastor at a church he'd never attended and live in a city he knew very little about.

Dam thought he had prayed and was assured that he was making the right decision for his future, but why the uneasy feeling today?

"Hey-Ho! Hey-Ho!" his brothers DeMarcus, Dee, and Dontae busted through the door as soon as he unlocked it. Their hands were in the air as they strutted around his small room as if they were doing a frat brother step show. "Hey-Ho! Hey-Ho!"

"I see y'all turned up already this morning," Dam told them.

"Go on somewhere with that, we just trying to celebrate you becoming a G today," As Dee spoke his hand movement resembled a man throwing up gang signs.

Dam knew that Dee was about that hood life. Which was the reason that he hadn't seen his brother in over three years. They were like the tale of two cities. Dam followed after God while Dee followed after their gangster grandfather. Even though Dam knew that his Pop-Pop wasn't right, he still loved the old man. Dam also loved Dee, but it was way past time to get him straight on some things. "I'm not trying to be no G, I'm a man of God, and that's all I've ever wanted. I hope you can respect that."

DeMarcus, the oldest of the four brothers, shook his head. "Dee wasn't calling you a G as in a gangster. He was saying that you a G as in a graduate."

"With Dee, you never know." Dontae laughed at the remark he made against his brother. Dam and DeMarcus laughed at Dee as well.

But Dam stopped laughing as he noticed that Dee was not amused by the joke. Dam wondered about the look in Dee's eye and was about to ask if everything was alright in his world but then the door flung open again, and Dodi strutted in.

"The princess has arrived, so let the party begin." Dodi took off her sunglasses and flung her hair around as if she was staring in a commercial featuring twelve- inch weave.

Dam shook his head at the antics of his sixteen- year- old baby sister. She was the youngest of the Shepherd children. Her name meant, 'Well Loved.' And Dodi made sure that each of her brothers lived up to their obligation to be kind and loving to her.

"Where is the king and queen who created this monster of a princess we all have to deal with?" Dam bent down and kissed his sister on the cheek. She might be a brat… but she was a well-

loved brat.

"They're parking the car. I didn't want them blocking any of these cute college guys from giving me them digits."

Dee menacingly glanced out of Dam's dorm room window. "Who? Which one of them dudes gave you their number? Whoever he is, he's got a statutory beatdown coming from me."

The rest of the brothers joined in on the beatdown threats until Dodi was forced to admit, "I didn't get any digits on the way up here, okay. Calm down, **boys.** This is supposed to be a Christian college. I doubt they'd like to see a brawl bust out on graduation day."

"Mom and Dad need to lock you in the house until you're twenty-five," Dontae said as he playfully nudged his sister.

"What's this I'm hearing?" Demetrius asked as he and Angel stepped into the room. "Why on earth would I need to lock my little princess away?"

Dodi stuck her tongue out at her brothers as she put an arm around her father's waist. "Told ya I

was a princess." Dee scowled at his sister as he proclaimed her, "Princess Hot-In-The-Pants."

Now Angel was scowling. "Good Lord, what have you gotten yourself into while we were parking the car."

"Nothing Mama. Dee is just being mean to me as usual."

"You're not fooling me, Dodi. I was once a sixteen- year- old girl myself, and I had plenty on my mind and whatin none of it holy." Angel wagged a finger at her daughter. "Watch yourself, young lady."

"Why are we focused on me?" Dodi pointed towards Dam. "Aren't we here for a graduation?"

Dam glanced at his watch. "We better get going, or I won't be able to line up with the rest of the grads."

Dam rushed everyone out of his room and locked the door. As they headed over to the auditorium for the graduation ceremony, Angel shed tears of joy. "This is such a happy day. My youngest son is all grown up and will soon be setting off into the ministry that God has for him."

Dam wished he felt the same way his mom did about the job he'd accepted as youth pastor in a little country town not far from where his mother's parents lived in Winston Salem, NC. But in truth Dam just didn't know for sure. He took the job because it had been the only one offered to him at the time. Ever since accepting that job offer, Dam had been praying, asking God to show him what his true calling in ministry would be.

But as he stepped off the stage after receiving his diploma, there was no more time for Dam to ponder his future. He noticed his father smiling while lifting his cell phone to his ear. Then moments later the expression etched upon his father's face was nothing short of pain and disbelief. Dam immediately knew that something had just happened that would forever change their world.

Instead of walking back to his seat with the other graduates, Dam rushed over to his father. "What is it, Dad? What happened?"

"Aren't you supposed to be sitting over there?" Dodi pointed to the empty seat next to two other guys in cap and gowns.

"Go back to your seat son. We'll talk later," Demetrius told him.

"No Dad. Tell me now. Something is wrong, and I need to know what it is."

Sighing deeply, Demetrius said, "It's your Pop-Pop. He wants to see you."

Pop-Pop was the name all the kids called their grandfather, the notorious gangster, Don Shepherd. Word on the street was, Don Shepherd had murdered hundreds of men. "I thought he was coming to my graduation. Where is he?" This was supposed to be the day that he would see his Pop-Pop again. His father had forced him to focus on his studies and made him promise not to come visit Pop-Pop or Dee until he was finished.

"He's in the hospital, Dam. It doesn't look good."

Demetrius averted his eyes as he said those words, and Dam knew why... this was all his fault. Dam would have a tough time forgiving his father if Pop-Pop died before he had a chance to introduce him to the man he'd spent all these years learning about.

1

Back in The Day - 1945

Don Shepherd was born on December 5, 1933, on the same day that devil juice, known as alcohol, became legal in most states. But just because Prohibition had been struck down, and his daddy would now have to get out of the moonshine business, that didn't mean the family would no longer be in the business of crime... just more organized crime.

The day Don turned twelve, reality slapped him in the face. Up until that day, he'd been living with his Mama in a brothel. While Don had understood exactly what his mother did with those men she took to her room, she made sure that he was occupied with his books and his football while she handled her business.

All of that changed when Leon Shepherd came storming through the house demanding to see his son. His mom, Starlight came busting out of her room, throwing a silk robe over her scantily clad voluptuous body. "No Leon, you can't do this. We had an agreement."

"Times up Starlight, my boy is old enough to come with me now, and that's what he's 'bout to do."

"I ain't never asked you for nothing, Leon… nothing. All I want is for my boy to grow up and be something."

Don came into the parlor tossing his football from one hand to the next. The first thing he noticed was the tears that were streaming down his mother's face. At that moment he realized that he'd never seen this street wise woman shed a tear for nothing. Why now?

"He is gon' be somethin.' I got big plans for this boy." Leon popped his collar like he was the man and everything coming after him was fake and irrelevant.

Starlight pointed at her son. "Look at him, Leon. The boy is built for football. His coach says he's got the best footwork he's ever seen."

Leon took a couple steps in Starlight's direction, his lip curled in a snarl as he said, "You trying to turn our son into another Kenny Washington. That boy is probably the greatest football player Negros have ever seen, and he can't get in the NFL. He ended up in the Pacific Coast League, and now he's off fighting this white man's war. And you're telling me, that's what you want for Don?"

"Kenny Washington is sure to get a spot in the NFL, then he'll crack the door wide open for Don. We just gotta give our boy a chance, Leon. We don't want him turning out like us."

Leon smacked Starlight so hard with the back of his hand that she fell down. "Speak for yourself. Cause ain't nothing wrong with my son turning out like his old man, is it Don?"

Don was on the floor next to his mother, wiping the blood from her lip. He wanted to attack his father every time the man put his hands-on Starlight. But he'd tried that once and gotten beat to a pulp for his pitiful efforts. Leon wasn't just meaner than a bear. He was big and burly and a former heavy weight boxer.

"Go get your clothes, boy. It's time for you to stop hanging out with these no-count hookers and work like a man."

"I'm not going… Staying here with Mama."

Leon lifted his big, black, haymaker sized hand again. "Don't back talk me, boy; you gon' do as I tell you."

"No!" Don stood up, balled his fist and set his feet. He'd take the beat down, but he wasn't leaving his mother without anyone to protect her from the men who treated her like she was just a piece of meat.

"Oh, so you're ready for this beating, huh?" Leon took the thick, spike laden belt off his pants. He stepped forward, grinning at Don as he reached down and grabbed hold of Starlight's hair and pulled her off the ground. "I bet your mama still got enough sense to be

15

terrified of one of my beatings. Want me to show you how scared she is?"

"Leave her alone." Don rushed at his daddy like a linebacker sacking a quarterback. But Leon had learned to bob and weave with the best of them, as he moved out of the way, he grabbed Don by the back of his neck and flung him to the ground.

Don was getting back up, about to charge at his daddy again, when he heard a God-awful scream. Leon had his mother by the neck now. Her eyes bugged out as if she was about to pass out.

Leon said, "Tell your son what time it is."

Starlight didn't say anything. Leon tightened his grip. "Tell him!"

"Go... go get your things, Donnie."

Don shook his head.

As Leon loosened his grip a bit, Starlight said, "It's time that you learn how to be a man. I can't teach you that, only your father can."

"Who is going to look out for you if I'm not here?" Don didn't care what she said, he knew she needed him. His mother was always so scared in the middle of the night. Don had caught her crying many times. He had been the one to put a smile back on her face.

But Starlight laughed at him. "Boy, you think you can protect me? If you don't go get your things, I'll use that belt your daddy is holding and whup you myself."

Leon released his hold on Starlight's neck. He shoved her toward Don. "Help the boy pack his things. I don't have all night."

"You heard him, Donnie. Let's go get your stuff." Starlight wiped away a few tears as she walked Don to his room and began packing his clothes.

"But Ma, I thought you said that I was good at football."

Starlight stopped folding her son's clothes and sat down on his bed. "Don't you let this stop you. You hear me, Donnie. You got a gift, and one day the NFL is going to let negroes in the league again. So, keep practicing and be ready."

~~~~

"But I don't want to go with daddy, Ma. I want to stay here and play football." Don was yelling and flailing from one side of the bed to the other.

"Pop-Pop, It's me, Dam." Dam shook his grandfather's shoulders, trying desperately to pull him out of whatever was tormenting him so bad that his body was thrashing from one side of the bed to the other. "Wake up, Pop-Pop, you're not with your dad. You're in the hospital, and we are here with you."

His words sounded strange to his ears. Dam had never known his grandfather to be scared of anything. During Dam's teenage years as he realized that his grandfather was the head of a powerful crime family, he had taken to calling him 'The Don' whenever he referred to his grandfather. But when he spoke directly to The Don he still called him Pop-Pop. Because Dam was too chicken to say that to his grandfather's face. The Don had always seemed bigger than life to him. And even though Dam knew that Jesus was much bigger… he still honored his grandfather with the respect he had earned on the streets.

But now as he watched The Don pull himself out of this nightmare that had him trying to get away from his dad, Dam didn't see the same man that had caused so many to fear and obey him through the years. Dam was looking at a very old and frail man, and he wondered when this had occurred. Dam talked to his Pop-Pop at least once a month, but he hadn't seen him since his eightieth birthday bash. His grandfather was now eighty-three years old, but honestly, The Don had never looked a day over sixty-five, until now.

Don focused his eyes on Dam. A smile crossed his lips as he placed a hand on Dam's cheek. "I knew you'd come see about your Pop-Pop."

"Of course, I'm here. Where else would I be on a day like today."

"Well, you did have that graduation. I hope I didn't mess things up too bad for you. I told Al not to call. I didn't want to upset your father."

Dam shook his head. "You should have told him to call us last night. The school could have mailed my degree certification."

"No, no, I didn't want to ruin your graduation," Don told him as he glanced around the room. "Where's your father?"

"He'll be here later, Pop-Pop," DeMarcus stepped forward trying to ease the pain Don might feel in knowing that his only son wanted nothing to do with him, even now. DeMarcus then let his hand sweep around the room, pointing at everyone. "But look, Pop-Pop. Everyone else is here. Mom, Dodi, Dee, Dontae and me and Dam. We all came to see about you."

"The whole gang, minus one, I see." Don smirked as he added, "I must be dying to get all of y'all in the room at the same time."

"Don't say things like that, Pop-Pop," Dee rushed to his grandfather's side. "You're not old enough to die yet. You've got plenty more living to do."

Don shook his head. "I wish that were true, grandson. But my body is telling me something altogether different."

"We're praying for you, Don. We know what the doctors are saying, but God is able to raise you up," Angel told him.

Don turned his head in the direction of Angel's voice. When he looked at her, his eyes watered. "I'm sorry Starlight, so, so sorry," he said and then drifted back to sleep.

~~~~

Dam felt awful for his grandfather. The man sounded downright miserable as he mistook his mother for some woman named Starlight. Whoever she was, Pop-Pop was in misery over the way he must have treated her.

19

He wanted to do something for his grandfather. Giving him something to take the blues away, so he went to the first floor in search of the gift shop. On his way, he passed an alcove type area that housed a row of pay phones. The area first caught his attention because he wasn't used to seeing pay phones these days... I mean, who didn't have a cell phone in 2018? The second reason the area caught his attention was because a woman was standing at one of the stations with her ear pressed to the phone, tears running down her face as she shouted at the person on the other end.

Dam didn't want to stick his nose where it didn't belong, but he was transfixed and couldn't move. He wanted to wipe the tears from her face. Pull her in his arms and hold her until the sadness drifted away.

"Why are you staring at me? Mind your own business," the woman yelled at Dam.

"I'm sorry, I didn't mean to stare. I only stopped because you seem so distraught. Can I help you." Maybe he should tell her that he was a minister. Maybe she wouldn't be so offended by a man of God sticking his nose where it didn't belong.

The woman didn't respond to Dam. She shouted into the phone. "I've got to get back to work... no, no, don't do that. I want nothing to do with you." She hung up the phone.

"You still here?" She barked at Dam as she walked toward him.

"I just want to help. God doesn't want you in pain like this. If you don't mind, I'd like to pray with you."

"Oh yeah right, God cares so much about me." She scoffed at him. "I don't need your prayers," she said as she stormed past him.

Dam watched her walk through the double doors of the ICU. She had on a pair of blue scrubs, so he figured she must work in this area of the hospital. Hopefully, she wouldn't take her problems out on her patients. The woman was gorgeous, but she had a serious attitude problem. He felt sorry for the poor guy on the other end of that phone.

2

1945

Leon Shepherd made some of his money selling moonshine to all those who thumbed their nose at the government for outlawing that so-called devil-juice when the devil-juice had been like a good old friend to them. It helped ease the pain of living through the worst depression the United States of America had ever known, and it helped ease the pain of being black in a white man's world. Thanks to the end of prohibition, Leon now owned a saloon where plenty of liquor was available, and the law couldn't touch him.

Don's daddy was proud that he'd beat a white man out of the saloon and nobody had been able to do anything about it because Leon had made that white man sign a contract that stated the amount he'd paid for the saloon. Leon had also hired a photographer to snap a picture of himself and the previous owner as they shook hands with mounds of cash on the table in front of them. The cashed was used to purchase the saloon, and the signed one-page contract had been placed on top of the cash.

It also helped that Leon had put the fear of God in the previous saloon owner, because when Leon fired the bartender to bring his own guy into the saloon, the old bartender ran to the police, claiming that Leon swindled the boss out of his saloon. The white man knew better than to mess with crazy Leon. He told the police that he had gambling debts and needed to get his house out of foreclosure before his wife and kids ended up on the street and that's why he sold to a nigger.

When Don first moved in with his dad, his job had been dish washing. The moment the school house opened the doors and turned him loose, Don high tailed it to the saloon and got to busting suds. His dad normally let him sit in the saloon when he finished with his chores. When he lived in the brothel, his mother never told him anything. The minute he asked questions about the men coming in and out of the house, he was told to mind his own business and to go outside and practice football.

But as Don watched the scantily clad women take men up the stairs and spend thirty minutes to an hour with them, he saw that his dad had the same racket going on in his saloon as he had at the brothel. His dad was pulling in big cash, and Don wanted to live good and drive good, just like his daddy was doing.

"See something you like," Leon smirked at his son as he sat down across from him.

Don leaned forward. "Dad, do you think those women like it when the men hang all over them and kiss them and stuff?"

Leon shrugged. "Don't matter."

"Huh?" Don couldn't wrap his thirteen-year-old mind around the concept of a woman's opinion not mattering, especially since his mama had raised him for the first twelve years of his life. And he heard her opinion on this and that all-day long.

"They do what I tell them to do. If they don't, then there's consequences and repercussions."

"Even mama?"

A vicious laugh escaped Leon's lips. "Now, your mama is different. She has always loved

hooking. That trollop wouldn't be able to hold a job that didn't require laying on her back. Why

you think she gave you up?"

"You took me from her."

Leon snapped his finger as if he just remembered something. "I take it back. With the performance your mama put on when I came to pick you up, she should have been an actress." He leaned back in

24

his seat and spread his hands out in front of his face. "I can see it now, Starlight the Amazing Hooker, coming to a theater near you."

"She wasn't acting." Don hated it when his dad riffed on his mom. Starlight didn't like being a prostitute. She had told him so herself. She'd even told him that they would get away from Leon one day.

"If she wasn't acting, then why did she beg me to take you off her hands just a week before I showed up to get you."

"She didn't." Don didn't believe it.

"Then why hasn't she come to visit you in all the time you've been here?"

His mom had stayed away an awfully long time. Don wasn't allowed to go back to the brothel, only customers, his dad had told him. But he had expected Starlight to come see him. Where was she?

Leon pointed at a woman whose face was painted with just enough of that face powder to cover the black eye she'd been sporting the past two nights. "It's time for Trista to make a man out of you."

At that moment, Trista was holding the hand of a very drunk, fowl mouthed man as she guided him up the stairs to one of the back rooms. Don didn't understand how Trista would be able to make him a man, but he knew that it had something to do with those back rooms upstairs. When the men came back downstairs after visiting one of those rooms, they were always smiling like they knew something the rest of the world didn't have a clue about. Yeah, he wanted to smile like that too.

~~~~

By the time Don saw his mother again, he had been to that back room upstairs with all the girls who worked at the bar. He was now fourteen and feeling man enough to visit the brothel he had grown up in. He walked in waving around ten-dollar bills. "I'm looking for a good time, ladies. Who wants to get paid?"

A woman who Don used to call Ms. Peaches gasped as she said, "Dear God, that's Starlight's boy."

"I'm nobody's boy, Peaches. I'm a man, and I brought my money. You up for the time of your life?"

"Boy, you better get your narrow behind out of here," Peaches told him.

A woman who Don didn't recognize stepped forward. "I'll take that money off your hands."

"You'll do no such thing, Jewel. You've only been here for a week, so you have no idea that this is Starlight's boy. Most of the girls in here changed his diapers, and I'm not getting ready to let him run through the women in this house," the house mother said.

"What do you care? My money is green just like the rest of the John's. And anyway, my daddy owns this joint... not you."

The house mother narrowed her eyes on Don as she stepped closer to him, hands on hips. "Your daddy may own this joint, as you put it... but I run it. And I said, your money don't spend in here. And why has it been two years since we've seen your narrow behind anyway?"

"My daddy said only paying customers could come up in here." Don waved the money in his hand as he spit the words out of his mouth.

"Well, in that case," the house mother took one of the tens out of his hand and then pointed towards Starlight's bedroom. "Go see your mother. She's been plum miserable without you."

Don was about to object. Starlight hadn't checked on him, not once in the years he'd been gone. He was even surprised that she was still in town. He thought she had left for that faraway place she used to tell him about when she dreamed of being a movie star. But then he caught the look the house mother gave him... like he was scum for not wanting to visit is mother. "Whatever." He tossed up his hands, walked over to Starlight's door and knocked.

"Go away," Starlight barked. "I don't work one minute before six o'clock. So, get off my door."

Did the house mother change the hours around this joint without letting his dad know? These hookers weren't allowed to kick back and relax until the evening. He banged on the door. "It's me, Don. Open the door, I want to talk to you."

He heard some kind of commotion in his mother's room. Like she got up, fell down, knock some stuff over and then got up again.

"What are you doing in there?"

"On my way," she said as she stumbled around the room. But her words sounded more like... Ooon myyy waaaayy.

His mother's voice didn't sound slurred as if she'd been drinking. But she was talking so slow that Don figured something had to be wrong. She opened the door. Don stepped in and closed the door behind him. Starlight reached out to hug him.

"My... booooy."

Don slipped out of her embrace and held his mother at arm's length. "What's wrong with you? Why do you sound like you're on some kind of delay?"

"Not... late." Starlight tried to swing around and do one of the poses she used to do to make Don laugh. But stumbled and almost fell.

Don sat his mother in a chair to keep her from getting hurt. But as Starlight sat down, her head bobbed back and forth as if she was nodding out. He'd seen men nod out like that a couple of times at his dad's bar. Leon told him that they were good-for-nothing junkies. Now he was staring at another junkie who just happened to be his mother.

"You ready to run away to Hollywood with me, Don? I've been waiting for you to come back so we could go."

"I'm not going anywhere with you," he shouted at her. "You're nothing but a junkie." He turned and ran out of the room, headed for the front door.

But the house mother stopped him. "Don't leave like this Don. Your mother needs you. She's sick."

"Yeah, I can see that."

"You were the one thing that she had in this world. Losing you destroyed her."

"Don't give me that crap. She was happy to be rid of me, now I see why." He flung the front door open and stormed out.

3

"Wake up, Pop-Pop, you're having another one of those dreams."
Dam had spent the night at the hospital with his grandfather while
the rest of the crew went home to get some rest. He hated watching
this man who had always seemed bigger than King Kong, the Hulk,
and the Transformers put together deteriorating right before his eyes.
But Dam couldn't imagine being anywhere else. His ministry, his
new job... all of it could wait until Don was back to himself again.

As gently as he could, Dam rocked his grandfather from side to
side, trying to get him to open his eyes so he could get away from
whatever was tormenting him as he slept. "Pop-Pop, it's Dam. Wake-
up and talk to me."

Don let out a loud hacking cough as his eyes sprang open and he
popped up as if he was trying to run away from something or
someone. His eyes darted around the room as he took in his
surroundings. He then laid his head back on his pillow and exhaled.
Glancing over at Dam he, said, "man, are you a sight for these old
eyes."

Dam laughed at that. "I remember when you threatened to take me over your knee for calling you an old man."

"That was ten years ago. I wasn't feeling like an old man then. But I'm losing this battle with Father Time." Don coughed, and his frail body shook.

Dam didn't like that his grandfather was talking about some mystical Father Time when he should recognize that it is God who numbers our days. Dam told him, "You know I love you, Pop-Pop and that I've never cared how you make your money or about you being in prison for all those years or none of the other stuff either."

Don reached his hand out and patted his grandson's arm. "You've always been my special one."

They had a connection. And Dam wouldn't trade his grandfather for anyone else. Sometimes his grandfather spouted off about things that were contrary to the word of God, and Dam had given him a pass. But if time was running out, he now owed Don the whole truth. "And that's why I can't let you talk like this without telling you that it's time to get right with God."

Don scoffed at that, then his face contorted in the most agonizing look of pain Dam had ever seen.

Dam jumped out of his seat. "What's happening? Pop-Pop, what's wrong?"

Don knocked the morphine drip as he pushed the button, sending hot flowing pain relief through his body. Exhaling as the pain subsided, he turned to his grandson and confessed, "God gave up on me a long time ago. I've done so much wrong in order to make my way in this world." Don shook his head, a hint of sorrow crossed his face. "It's good enough that the man upstairs hasn't turned his back on my family. That's good enough for me."

"But Pop-Pop, listen to me. God wants to save you too. He wants our whole family to know the joy of living for Him."

Don shook his head. He patted his grandson's arm. "There's no redemption for a man like me."

Dam was getting ready to tell his grandfather about the good God that he served. A forgiving God who sent His son Jesus for the sins of the world, but Don's eyes closed as he went into full snore mode. Discouraged, Dam slumped over to the window and looked up to heaven. With a heavy heart, he asked the Lord, "How can I ever convince others that You can save and deliver them if I can't get my own grandfather to believe it?"

~~~~

"Why are you torturing yourself like this?" Angel asked Demetrius. "You know you want to be at the hospital with Don, but you keep putting it off."

"I told you, I don't want to talk about this."

Angel hated when her husband took 'The Tone' with her. The tone that signaled the discussion was over whether she was finished talking or not. And she rarely let him get away with it. With one hand on her hip, she scolded, "I'm not the enemy, Mr. Shepherd. I'm on your team, so you're just not gon' talk to me in that tone of voice."

Shaking his head as if trying to get something off him, Demetrius walked over to his wife. "You are absolutely right, Mrs. Shepherd. Trust me, I will never forget that we are on the same team." He lowered his head and touched his lips to hers.

Smiling, because for the last ten years she and her husband have truly been on the same team. They laughed together, sat down to dinner together, prayed together and worshipped together because they were both on God's team now. It was a beautiful thing, so Angel was more than willing to let Demetrius off the hook for being a bit snippy with her. In fact, the only reason she wouldn't drop the issue all together was because she knew why he was being so short with her lately. Putting a hand on his arm, she asked, "Are you ready to deal with what's bothering you?"

The phone rang, Demetrius lifted his index finger to his wife's lips as he picked up the receiver. "What's up old man, I wondered when we'd hear from you. I know it's warm in Florida, but you could at least visit us in the summer months."

"I'm on my way there as we speak. Your father taking ill is the only thing that could make me leave this warm weather. But that's not why I'm calling," Al said and then sighed deeply before continuing.

Demetrius had been smiling, but as the person on the other end talked, his smile waned. He then turned his back to Angel. Thinking Demetrius was trying to get away from her so he wouldn't have to finish their conversation, Angel folded her arms and declared, "You're not getting off the hook that easy. When you hang up the phone, I'm still going to be standing right here." Her face was set, and she was determined to wait him out. But when Demetrius turned back to face her, without uttering a word. Angel knew that trouble was brewing for the Shepherd family again.

"Dee's been rushed to the hospital."

"What? Who were you just talking too?"

"Al."

"Al lives in Florida. How does he still know what's going on in Ohio?" Angel grabbed her coat and purse ready to leave the house. Dee had been acting out for most of his life, but he was still her son, and she loved him just as much as she loved her other children. She'd been praying for him and was patiently waiting for God to open her son's eyes to the truth. "What happened to him, Demetrius... and don't keep anything from me. We're in this together, remember?" When Demetrius was in the life, he kept a lot of things from her... and Angel could admit that there were a lot of things she didn't want to know about back then. But things were different now.

Demetrius took his keys off the hook in the mud room. "From what Al said, Dee overdosed. One of his boys found him with the needle in his arm."

Angel shook her head as she backed away from Demetrius. He dropped the keys and reached for his wife. "No, Demetrius. God wouldn't allow this to happen. Not now. Not now." Angel had recently talked with her son about turning his life over to the Lord. Dee had been receptive to the conversation and had even said, "I'm listening, Ma." Which was more than she'd ever gotten out of him when discussing salvation.

She thought that she'd heard God clearly tell her that all her children would serve the Lord, now her husband was saying that one of their sons had OD'd.

"Come on bae, let's get to the hospital so we can check on him."

But Angel was still shaking her head. Al doesn't even live here anymore. There's no way he could be sure about Dee. Maybe Al heard wrong, or Demetrius misunderstood. Al had been Don's enforcer for over fifty years until he finally retired and moved to Florida. Al wasn't even in the business anymore... was he?

Demetrius pulled Angel into his arms. "It's going to be alright, baby. Aren't you always telling me to trust God."

"I do trust Him. But now you're telling me that my son OD'd. That doesn't sound like the God that I trust."

4

"How's he doing, doctor?" Demetrius asked as he and Angel stood in the waiting room of the ICU.

With a somber look on his face, the doctor informed them, "I'm going to be honest with you. We were able to revive your son, but he's very weak. If he makes it through the night, then we'll know."

"Know what?" Angel wanted to grab hold of the collar on the doctor's white coat and implore him to give them a better prognosis right here and now. She didn't want to be on some death watch throughout the night. She wanted to know for sure that Dee was going to live and that he was going to turn his life around. But it wasn't the doctor's fault that her son had taken drugs and nearly killed himself.

"We'll know whether his heart will recover from the damage done to it," the doctor said and then walked away from them.

Angel sighed deeply, shook her head, then started talking to her heavenly father. Being married to Demetrius Shepherd had brought her both joy and sorrow, but through it all, God had been her refuge.

After all these years, Angel still clearly remembered the very first time she had turned to her Lord and Savior for refuge. She and Demetrius had only been married three years at the time. Their love was new, fresh and growing. Back then Angel couldn't imagine that anything could tear them apart. But then Demetrius and Don got arrested and needed bail money. She'd gone to an ex-boyfriend, her first born son's so-called 'real' father and asked him for help. Her plea for help to Frankie Day turned out to be the worst mistake she'd ever made in life. Frankie raped her. Soon after that Angel discovered that she was pregnant. Demetrius had stood by her side and comforted her after discovering that Frankie had put his hands on her, but the one thing he couldn't do was accept another man's child, not with the circumstances being what they were, so he had demanded that she have an abortion.

Angel didn't want another child by Frankie either, she couldn't be sure that the baby she was carrying belonged to Demetrius, so she made the appointment at the abortion clinic. For many years, Angel had been ashamed that her first encounter with God as an adult took place at an abortion clinic, but she had been a sinner through and through back then. Even though she had been raised by God fearing parents who taught her that abortion was wrong, Angel hadn't had any kind of relationship with God since she was fourteen years old.

She thanked God that the prayers of the righteous still get through to Him, because that marvelous day, in her darkest hour when she reached out to God, still causes her heart to sing...

The day finally came when Angel could take no more. She desperately wanted her husband to love her and for her family to be the tight knit unit they'd once been. She just wasn't strong enough to fight Demetrius one more day. So, she got in her car and drove down to the clinic on the east side of town, hoping that she wouldn't run into anyone she knew.

She pulled into the lot and checked the time. Her appointment was scheduled for 9 a.m. She was twenty minutes early, so she sat in her car and took a few deep breaths. Taking the key out of the ignition, Angel looked out at the street, and that's when she noticed the people holding picket signs.

One sign said, 'Don't Kill Your Baby... Every Life Matters.' Then another sign had on it, 'Jeremiah 1:5'.

The scripture was not written on the poster, but it didn't have to be. It was the same scripture her father used to read to her when she was a child: Before I formed you in the womb I knew you; Before you were born I sanctified you.

As the words of Jeremiah shocked her system, Angel once again realized why she thought of abortion as murder. Because if God knew a child and could sanctify him or her before they were even born, then the so-called fetus had to be a living thing. Angel was undone. All she had done was love a man who loved her and their family more than anything else. But life had dealt them a blow, now she didn't know what to do, or how to choose right rather than wrong.

Tears were blurring her eyes as the woman who'd been holding the 'Every Life Matters' poster knocked on her door. Angel wiped her face and rolled down the window.

The woman asked, "Would you like to talk to someone?"

Angel nodded as she unlocked the door and allowed the woman to get in the car.

The woman extended her hand. "I'm Patricia Miller-Harding. You don't have to cry anymore because God sent me here for you."

"Why would God send you to me?"

"You don't believe me?" Patricia put a gentle hand on Angel's shoulder as she said, "I know everything about you, Angel."

"How do you know my name?"

"God has given me a glimpse into your life… I know that your upbringing was all about the Lord and growing closer to Him. Until your parent's divorce, you had even planned to go into the ministry yourself. But then you ran away, moved in with a street wise guy, and when he tossed you out, instead of humbling yourself and going back to your parents, who had re-married, you started stripping, and then you fell in love with another criminal. You married him, now he has you here, about to kill one of God's soldiers."

"Who are you?" were the only words Angel could form. She was stunned that this woman could read her so well. What was going on?

"I'm a friend, sent by the Lord with a message for you."

"What's the message," Angel asked, still feeling a little devastated by the way she'd just been read.

Patricia looked directly into Angel's eyes and held onto her hands as she said, "Thus says the Lord, you were born to serve God, you chose not to... but this baby you are carrying will not be swayed by the enemy. He will do great and mighty things for the Lord."

Angel bowed her head as tears rolled down her face. When she was a little girl, she used to stand behind a makeshift podium preaching her heart out to the kids in the neighborhood. Her dad had told her that God had a calling on her life. She had believed it then. But when her dad hadn't been able to hold onto his own calling, Angel let hers slip away.

As she grew older, Angel began to think that so much more was out there in the world and that she was missing out on the good life by serving the Lord. But in truth, she had left the good life and was now suffering dearly for it. But her children didn't have to suffer, and they could grow to be much better human beings than she and Demetrius ever dreamed of being.

Angel turned her attention back to Patricia. She seemed like such a God-fearing woman, and her eyes were kind. So, Angel prayed that she could answer one question for her... because the answer to this question would solve all her problems. "God has told you all this stuff about me, right?"

Patricia smiled. "The Lord loves you."

She wanted to scream at Patricia, then where was he when Frankie attacked me? But instead, she asked, "Then tell me this, is the baby I'm carrying Demetrius' son?"

Without hesitation, Patricia told her, "The baby you're carrying will grow to be a great man of God. And God shall be his father."

That was an awesome thing for her child, but it still wasn't the answer she needed.

Patricia then said, "Go see KeKe, she is waiting at her house for you with another message from the Lord."

KeKe was Angel's best friend. KeKe was also a Christian woman. Angel almost asked Patricia how she knew about KeKe, but this woman was a messenger from God, so she knew because God told her. Angel turned to Patricia to tell her that she would go see KeKe, but she was no longer seated in her car, the woman had just disappeared. Angel sat there a moment looking around outside, Patricia was nowhere to be seen. Then she checked her watch.

It was 9 o'clock, time for Angel's appointment. But she couldn't get out of the car. Demetrius would hate her for this, but she wasn't going to kill her baby. She was going to birth him, love and care for him and sit back and wait to see the man he turned out to be. Pulling away from the abortion clinic, Angel headed for KeKe's place.

41

When she arrived, she got out of her car and slowly walked to her friend's door. She hadn't told KeKe about the baby, so she didn't know how she was going to approach the subject about whether or not she had a word from the Lord for her. Angel certainly wasn't going to admit that she had run into a woman at an abortion clinic.

Before she could knock on the door, KeKe swung it open. Her keys were in her hand. "Angel, what are you doing here?"

"Are you going somewhere?" Angel asked, avoiding the question.

"I'm headed back to the restaurant. I drove all the way down there this morning but forgot the key to unlock the door, so I had to come back home to get them."

Was it just a coincidence that KeKe had come back home and that Angel had arrived at her house right before she left again? Angel didn't know what was going on, but God had finally gotten her attention. She silently prayed, "Lord, lead and guide me. I'm ready to follow You again. Just tell me what You want me to do."

At that moment KeKe snapped her finger as if she had forgotten something. "It's funny that you showed up here this morning because I was going to come by your house when I finished working tonight."

"Really, what for?"

"I was reading in my Bible this morning, and the strangest thing happened. I know you probably won't believe me, but it felt like an angel directed me to a passage that was meant just for you."

"You'd be surprised," Angel told her. "Do you mind showing me that passage?"

Angel and KeKe stepped into the house. KeKe grabbed her Bible and opened it to Exodus 34:10 and began to read: "Behold, I make a covenant. Before all your people I will do marvels such as have not been done in all the earth, nor in any nation; and all the people among whom you shall see the work of the Lord. For it is an awesome thing that I will do with you."

"What does it mean?" KeKe asked once she finished reading, but Angel couldn't answer her because she was on the floor bowed down, praising God and giving Him all the glory for what He was about to do in her life.

"God is good... God is good," Angel kept saying over and over again. She wasn't afraid anymore. She knew what she had to do and where her loyalties must lie for this moment forward.

She went home and packed several bags and put them in the trunk of the car. Angel sat down and wrote Demetrius a note. She then got in her car, picked up her children from school and headed South with them.

All those years ago, she had been willing to leave Demetrius, the man who had captured her heart, for the sake of saving the life of her youngest son. God showed her that the child's life had been worth it because Dam is a true servant of God. He also, as it turned out was

Demetrius' son. Angel and Demetrius eventually reunited, and the family survived… or did it? Because somewhere along the way, they lost Dee. Now as Angel paced the floor of the ICU unit, praying and asking God to save yet another son from destruction, she wondered if she and Demetrius could have done more as parents for their wayward son.

5

The minute Dam heard about Dee, he fell on his knees and prayed until pellets of sweat dripped from his head, and yet he continued praying even as the sweat mixed with his tears. Dam could blame no one but himself. Even the Lord had convicted him earlier as he read the Word.

Dam had opened his Bible to the book of Matthew, Chapter 5. He smiled, thinking about how much he enjoyed reading the B-Attitudes… Blessed are the poor in spirit… blessed are the meek and so on. He delighted in these scriptures because they always encouraged him about his walk with the Lord. But then when he read versus 13-16 he knew exactly what the Lord was revealing to him:

"You are the salt of the earth. But if the salt loses its saltiness, how can it be made salty again? It is no longer good for anything, except to be thrown out and trampled underfoot.

You are the light of the world. A town built on a hill cannot be hidden. Neither do people light a lamp and put it under a bowl. Instead, they put it on its stand, and it gives light to everyone in the house. In the same way, let your light shine before others, that they may see your good deeds and glorify your Father in heaven."

He had turned a blind eye to the dirty dealings that went on in his family, he'd wanted to be accepted by them and not seen as some Jesus freak who pounded on the Bible every time they saw him. He had dimmed his light to make others in his family feel comfortable around him. But since he hadn't been back home in the past three years, it was more like, Dam had left his grandfather and brother in utter darkness rather than just dimmed a light. In doing so, he had denied them the truth that could change their lives. Dam was now devastated that in the midst of his silence his brother and his grandfather now lay dying. Anger was building in his heart because it didn't have to be like this.

"Help me, Lord, I made a terrible mistake. I listened to my earthly father when I should have been listening for the voice of my heavenly father. Please don't let me be too late, God. I don't know how I can live with what I've done if You don't give me a chance to make this right." He continued praying for a few minutes more. Hoping that he would hear something from God that would encourage him that everything was going to be alright. But only

46

silence filled his ears, and it was time for him to get to the hospital. He got off his knees, wiped the tears from his eyes, and left the house.

As he drove down the street, his cell phone rang. He didn't feel like talking, but when he saw the name Danny Short, he decided to answer it. Danny had been his prayer partner since his first year of college. "Hey man, what's going on."

"Nothing much going on over here. I haven't talk to you since graduation, so I'm just checking to make sure everything is good on your end."

"I thought about calling you or the Chaplin, but things have gotten crazy here."

"We have evening prayer at church later tonight, is there something I can ask everyone to pray about?"

Danny was an awesome friend and Dam was grateful that they were prayer partners. "Thank you, Danny. Yes, please pray. I'm on my way back to the hospital to see about my brother."

"I thought your grandfather was the one in the hospital?"

Nodding as if Danny could see him, Dam said, "My grandfather is in the hospital. He's not doing well at all. But my brother was just rushed to the hospital. From what I was told, he OD'd. I didn't even know he had a problem with drugs, that's how out of touch I've been. I feel terrible right now, man. Like I abandoned my family these last few years."

"Don't blame yourself for this, Dam. You've been away at school. God has been preparing you for ministry."

"Yeah, but what have I been doing while I've been at school? You and I both received all this Bible teaching, are we just learners or are we supposed to apply some of what we've learned?"

He was silent for a moment, but then he simply asked him, "Do you remember the story of the fig tree?"

"The one Jesus cursed for not bringing forth fruit?" Is that what Danny thought of him, that he was not performing as expected so he should be cut down? Was the Lord pruning him out of the ministry?

"No, not that one, the other fig tree."

He shook his head. "I don't remember another story about a fig tree."

In Luke Chapter 13 it says, "A certain *man* had a fig tree planted in his vineyard, and he came seeking fruit on it and found none. Then he said to the keeper of his vineyard, 'Look, for three years I have come seeking fruit on this fig tree and find none. Cut it down; why does it use up the ground?' But he answered and said to him, 'Sir, let it alone this year until I dig around it and fertilize *it*. And if it bears fruit, *well*. But if not, after that you can cut it down.'"

That scripture was not encouraging to Dam. "So, what if this is my final year to bear fruit and I mess everything up?"

"I'll be praying for you, man. God will show you His will in this situation."

"Thanks for calling, Danny. And I appreciate the prayers." They hung up, Dam continued driving down the street with a heavy heart. There were no more words left to justify his actions. How could it be okay to go off and prepare for ministry while the family he left behind fell apart? God couldn't be pleased with his actions, and neither was he. As he pulled into the hospital parking lot, Dam decided he would no longer be silent and complicit about his family's illegal lifestyle. Maybe if he could get them to see the error of their ways, God wouldn't allow anymore destruction to come to his family... at least, not for a long, long time.

He got out of the car and rushed into the Intensive Care Unit. His mom was crying, but she hugged him the moment he stepped into the waiting room. He wiped the tears from her face. "Don't cry, Mama; Dee will be alright. We just have to trust God on this one."

Angel blurted out, "He just had a seizure, and his blood pressure keeps dropping. The doctors don't know if your brother is going to make it through the night."

"What? But I thought they had revived him." Dam wasn't prepared for the news he just received. He trusted God with his whole life... with his every prayer. How could his brother have had a seizure in the space of time it took him to get to the hospital. Dam hadn't rushed out the door, he took the time to get on his knees and pray for his brother and grandfather before coming to the hospital.

Because Dam believed that God was the best doctor, the only doctor that they would ever need.

"There were complications," Demetrius said with a deep sigh as he walked over to them.

Dam swung around to face his father. "There shouldn't be any complications, Dad. Because none of this would have happened if you hadn't made me stay away from my family." Dam was done holding his anger in. His father was going to know exactly how he felt about this situation. Dam still remembered sitting in his dorm room with his bags packed waiting on his parents to pick him up so he could spend Christmas at home…

"What took you so long. I was beginning to think that I would have to walk to Ohio," Dam said as Demetrius came into his dorm room.

Demetrius walked over to the small two-seater table in Dam's eating area and sat down. "Come join me, son."

"My bags are packed." Dam glanced at his watch. "We need to get going because I'm supposed to meet Pop-Pop for dinner tonight."

"Have a seat Dam."

The look on his father's face told Dam that he wasn't getting out of this dorm room without first having a conversation with his dad. Dam sat down. "What gives, Dad? You're already late, I don't want to miss my dinner with Pop-Pop. I haven't seen him since his eightieth birthday bash at the end of the summer."

"You've been away at school, taking care of your studies. You don't need to concern yourself with your grandfather." 'Grandfather' sounded like a curse word as his father gritted out the word. "And I've already told him that you won't be having dinner with him tonight."

"What?" Dam's brow lifted in confusion. He and his Pop-Pop had always been close, they talked on the phone and hung out when Pop-Pop could pull himself away from business. He'd done lunch or dinner, hung out at the mall and gone fishing with his grandfather for years. Never once had his father objected or gotten in the way of his relationship with The Don, why now? "Why would you tell Pop-Pop that we can't have dinner? You've never had a problem with us hanging out before."

"Things have changed, Son. All I can tell you is your mother and I have both decided that you need to stay as far away from Pop-Pop as possible."

"What do you mean... things have changed? I know what Pop-Pop does. Why do you think I call him The Don? Just because he's a criminal that doesn't mean that I have to stop loving him. He's your father after all. Don't you love him?"

Demetrius didn't answer that. "Your mother and the rest of the family are in Winston Salem, North Carolina waiting on us. We will spend your Christmas break with your mother's parents this year."

"What about my summer break? Am I able to come home this summer?"

Demetrius shook his head. "I can't make any promises. Things have gotten complicated, and we are praying and asking God for guidance, but neither your mother nor I want you mixed up in all the drama that surrounds the Shepherd family. We want you to grow into the man that God designed you to be. Do you hear me, Son?"

Dam heard his father, but he didn't understand. It wasn't until he arrived at his grandparents' home in Winston Salem and greeted his mother and grandparents, DeMarcus, Dontae, and Dodi; that he realized that Dee would not be joining them. "Where is Dee?" He asked and then witnessed tears fall from his mother's eyes just before she turned and walked out of the room.

Dam swung around to face off with his Dad. "So, I guess I'm supposed to stay away from Dee also? Who else are you planning to purge from my life?"

"I'm not trying to hurt you, Dam. I wish things were different but right now they just aren't." Demetrius headed out of the room to go comfort his wife.

"Can anybody tell me what's going on around here?" Dam demanded.

DeMarcus put an arm around Dee's shoulder. "Take a walk with me, little bro." They headed out of the house and down the street toward an open field. Half way there, DeMarcus turned to Dam and told him, "Dee started working for Pop-Pop about a month after you left for college."

"What kind of working is he doing?"

"He's Pop-Pop's right hand man. So naturally, Mom and Dad aren't happy with Pop-Pop or Dee at this point."

"Tell me about it." Dam shook his head. "Dad won't even let me come back home for a visit."

"He's just worried that Pop-Pop will get you caught up in the so-called family business and cause you to lose focus on becoming like Billy Graham or any of them other great evangelists. God's got something special planned for you, Dam. We all see it, Dad doesn't want anything to get in your way."

"If spending time with Pop-Pop will cause me to leave the ministry and go into a life of crime then how can anyone believe that I was truly called by God?" There was a time in Dam's life that he felt closer to his Pop-Pop than he did to his own father. Demetrius wanted nothing to do with Dam until around the age of four. But before that time, Pop-Pop took an interest in him and made him feel like he belonged in the Shepherd family.

"You were too young to remember, but before dad gave his life to the Lord, he had been Pop-Pop's right hand man. He ran the crime *family business all while mom kept praying for him. But when Dad was a kid, he wanted to be a baseball player. He broke an ankle during a game, while he was recuperating and thinking about getting back to the field, Pop-Pop told him that he couldn't go back to baseball. He told him he'd never be any good at baseball again, so he was joining the family business."*

Dam was surprised at what he was hearing. "How could he know whether or not he'd be good at it if he didn't try? I can't believe that Pop-Pop wouldn't even let him try?"

"He was different with Dad than he is with us, Dam. Dad never had a choice. But he kept all of us away from the business and promised Mama that none of his sons would follow in his footsteps." DeMarcus shrugged his shoulders. "Somehow Dee got away from him, I don't think Dad will ever forgive himself for that."

"And now he's scared that Pop-Pop might recruit another one of his sons."

"Exactly!" DeMarcus lifted his hands with a look on his face that said, 'the boy finally gets it.' "So, give Dad a break and listen to him on this one."

Dam had listened to his father, he had stayed away for three years, but that hadn't made anything better for his Pop-Pop or for Dee. Their lives were now in ruin, he wasn't staying away one second longer. "You can't stop me from seeing him. You're not getting your way this time, Dad."

"Calm down, Son. The doctor will be back out here to speak with us. I already asked the nurse to go get him."

Dam's hands went to his head as his eyes darted around the waiting room. "What are we doing out here? We should be in there with Dee."

"Agreed," Demetrius said to his youngest son. "That's why I sent for the doctor. We need his approval to get back there with your brother. Believe me Dam, we are doing all that we can for Dee. We're not just going to sit here and let him die without fighting every step of the way."

Taking a deep breath, Dam leaned his head back, closed his eyes for a second. When he opened them again, the nurse was rushing over to them. "Follow me," she said. "The doctor says it's okay for you to see your son now."

Demetrius grabbed Angel's hand and followed behind the nurse. As they reached the entry to the ICU, the nurse noticed that Dam was also following, she lifted a hand. "Sorry, only immediate family."

Dam and the nurse locked eyes. He recognized her immediately. The gorgeous nurse with the bad attitude. He wasn't putting up with her mess today. "I'm his brother." Dam looked as if he wanted to pound his chest. "You can't stop me from seeing him."

The nurse was about to deny Dam, but Angel put a hand on the woman's arm, her eyes implored the nurse. "Please, we just want to be with Dee. Let my son see his brother, okay."

The nurse didn't respond, she just turned and kept walking, when they reached Dee's room, she pointed towards the door. "All of you can go in, but try not to make too much noise, so I don't get in trouble for this, okay."

"Thank you," Dam said as he and his parents entered Dee's room.

The nurse followed them in. She wrote her name on the black board and then told them, I'm Nurse Harris. If you need anything, just hit the nurse button."

Dam fixed his eyes on his brother. He didn't know what he had expected to see, but his brother was laying so still in that hospital bed with IVs in his arm, tubes in his nose and monitors beeping all around the room that it spooked him.

His mother traced her fingers up the length of Dee's arm. She stopped as she came upon a few puncture holes. She turned to Demetrius, "Did you know he had these puncture marks on his arm?"

"No baby, I didn't know Dee was shooting up. I wouldn't have kept something like that from you." He looked at his son's arm. "There are only a few marks, so hopefully he just started doing this stuff."

56

Dam looked over his mother's shoulder at Dee's arm and began to weep. "I knew something was wrong with him when he came to my graduation... but I ignored it because I thought it was nothing more than Dee being out of control as usual." Dam put a hand on Dee's leg as he told him through tears, "I'm sorry I turned my back on you, brother. Please forgive me."

Within seconds nurses and doctors ran into the room as Dee's monitors beeped uncontrollably. "He's seizing again!" one of them yelled.

6

"No God, no! This isn't happening. I won't let it happen." As his brother spasmed and doctors and nurses tried to get Dam and his parents out of the room, so they could handle business their way, Dam shook them off and refused to be moved.

He lifted his head to God in prayer, and in that moment God revealed to him what was happening to his brother. The doctor's wouldn't be able to help Dee, he had to do it. Dam pushed his way back to the bed, moving hospital personnel out of the way.

One of them shouted, "Call for security." The others in the room grabbed hold of Dam and continued pushing him back. All the while Dee's body was being flung from one side of the bed to the other.

"No!" Angel shouted back. "Leave my sons alone. Let him get to his brother."

Dam prayed for strength. Two men had his left hand pinned to his body, his father yanked them away from him, then Dam reached out and placed that hand on Dee's chest. "In the name of Jesus, I command you to come out!" Dam spoke to the unclean spirit that dwelled in his brother's body trying to wreak havoc and destroy him.

Commotion was going on all around the room. But at that moment Dee stopped convulsing and was completely still, like a dead man.

Angel screamed. "God help him!"

Dee then opened his eyes and sat up in the bed. Once he sat up, all commotion stopped, and the room was completely silent for what seemed like hours, but it had only been a few moments before one of the nurses glanced over at the doctor and asked, "You gave him the shot?"

The doctor shook his head and held up the syringe. "I didn't get a chance to."

"Then what happened?" Another doctor asked incredulously.

"Dee put a hand on his head as he looked around the room with a confused look on his face. "What's going on? Why am I in the hospital?"

Angel shouted, "Thank you, Jesus!" as she and Demetrius rushed toward the bed.

Dam, feeling weak and as if he might pass out, found the nearest chair and sat down. At that point, security showed up at the door, but he watched as one of the doctors waved them off. "Everything's okay in here. The disturbance has ended, let's just let these people spend a little more time with the patient."

"But I need to take his vitals," Nurse Harris demanded.

It was obvious the doctor had lost interest. "Look, didn't you just hear these people thank Jesus. They don't need us in here, but go ahead and take the vitals if it will make you feel better. I've got other patients to see... the ones that need doctors rather than some mystical God."

When the doctor and the other hospital personnel stepped out of the room, the nurse checked Dee's oxygen level and his blood pressure.

Dee winked at the nurse. "When'd they start hiring nurses as fine as you? Over there looking like Gabrielle Union. My, my, my, I'm gon' need them digits before I get released from this place."

She didn't respond to Dee as she put her equipment away, but there was a bewildered expression on her face.

"You look worried. What's wrong?" Demetrius asked her.

"Well... nothing, I guess. But that's what confuses me." She shook her head as if shaking away thoughts she didn't want to clutter her head. Then she turned back to the family. "Look, I know what the doctor said about y'all being able to stay in the room. But if your son truly is on the mend, then he's going to need some rest. So, do you mind stepping out for a while?"

Demetrius took Angel's hand in his. "Of course, we can step out. We want Dee to get better. We're not here to get in the way of that."

Angel leaned down and kissed Dee on the forehead. "Get some rest son. We'll be back to see you in a little while."

"But I'm not tired," Dee proclaimed.

"You will be," Nurse Harris told him. "You're running on adrenaline right now, but your body will crash before you know it. Seizures take a lot out of the body so please just rest for a few hours."

"Listen to your nurse, Dee. We'll go sit with Pop-Pop for a little while then come hang out with you later." Dam stood up and followed his parents out of the room.

But when Dam headed toward the elevators that would take him to Don's room. Demetrius exploded. "I forbid you to go anywhere near that man."

Dam swiveled around to face his father. "You forbid me to what?"

"You heard me. That man is the reason Dee almost died. I want you as far away from him as possible."

"Dad, 'That man' you are referring to is your father. And you have forbidden me to see him and Dee for the last time. I won't separate myself from them any longer and neither should you."

"Why are we arguing?" Angel put a hand on Demetrius arm. "Your son is alive. And your father is dying. Don't you think it's time to forgive… before it's too late."

Demetrius' jaw set in anger. "I'll never forgive him. If it had only been me who he recruited into his so-called family business, then maybe I could have forgiven him, because I am finally out. But when he turned my son." Demetrius shook his head. "I can't forgive that, Angel."

"But you can't cause us all to turn our back on Don. I know what he did, but I also know Dee, so I can't lay it all at Don's feet." Angel understood her husband's anger, but she could not and would not continue to live with it in her heart anymore. Don had done horrible things to their family, but even in that, he still qualified for God's forgiveness.

"Y'all can forgive him then." Demetrius waved them off. "I'm going to the cafeteria."

Angel told Dam, "Go see about your Pop-Pop. When you're done with your visit meet your father and me in the cafeteria."

"Okay, Mom and thanks for understanding."

"I understand where you're coming from, Son. But, do you understand where your dad is coming from... give him a little grace too." After saying that Angel rushed to catch up with Demetrius.

~~~~

Don had caused much harm to men, women, and children in the years since he went into the family business with his father. In all the years since he'd done his first dirty deed or even after he'd made his first kill, Don hadn't regretted much. But as Al sat across from him telling him that his grandson was laid up in the very same hospital he was in because he OD'd, Don knew then what regret felt like. His eyes filled with unshed tears. "Why did we let Dee in the business in the first place. He might be Demetrius' name sake, but that boy has never had the right mind set like his daddy and me."

Al hung his head. "You can blame it all on me, Don. From the bottom of my heart, I'm sorry for doing this to you, man. I knew you didn't want Dee in the business, but he kept coming at me, and I was ready to retire, so I figured you wouldn't mind letting me out if you had one of your grandsons in the business with you."

Don shook his head. "You're my oldest and dearest friend. How can I blame you for wanting to get out of the business when you've been through so many wars with me?"

Al leaned back and grinned at that. "Heck, we started a lot of those wars ourselves."

Don chuckled. "And took the spoils like they were our birthright."

"Dang skippy, we did. And dared anybody to stop us."

"You know what I would do right now if I wasn't confined to this bed." Don's eyes filled with malice. "I'd find the idiot who sold Dee that heroine, and I'd gut him."

"I'm not confined to no hospital bed. I can go find him."

"No, old friend. I was just speaking from my heart. But we both know that our days of ruling the streets are over."

"Thank God you figured that out, old man." Dam had been standing at the door listening in on his grandfather's conversation. He'd heard enough.

"Who you calling old?" Al bald his fist and punched the air like he was getting ready for a fight.

"You." Dam pointed at Al, then at Don. "And you. Listen at y'all, in here plotting on somebody else instead of resting in your old age. When is it time to stop doing crime?"

"Don't be upset with your Pop-Pop. Al and I were just talking foolishness. Come in here and tell us about Dee. How is he doing?"

"He kept having seizures, but we prayed for him, and he's doing much better now. He was woke, and talking when the nurse asked us to leave the room for a little while so he could rest."

"Now that's something to thank the Lord for. Good God, my grandson, is alive!"

Al even stood up and lifted his hands in praise. "I was so worried about that boy. Thank God they were able to revive him."

"Yes, we certainly want to thank God for that. But I have a question for the two of you." Dam sat down and looked from Al to his grandfather. "The two of you were just talking about what you wanted to do to the man who sold Dee those drugs, but the real question is what do you think should be done to you? Because it's likely that Dee stole those drugs from your stash."

Don was silent for a moment. But when he lifted his head and looked Dam in the eye, he said, "Then I guess dying is the best thing that I can do for this family."

7

As he walked to the cafeteria, Dam had a heavy heart. He didn't mean to condemn his grandfather like that, but hearing the two men talk and laugh about committing crime made him feel some kind of way. His father had dealt with this kind of behavior from The Don all his life. His mother had asked him to give his father a little grace and try to understand where he was coming from, after hearing Pop-Pop and Al brag about the good ol' days, he was beginning to understand his father.

Dam didn't agree that they needed to stay away from Don because of the way he was, but he understood why his father wanted nothing else to do with Don. He planned to tell his father exactly that when he sat down with his parents in the cafeteria. But he couldn't find them. They must have eaten and gone back to the waiting area.

He would catch up with his parents later. His stomach was growling, so Dam went through the cafeteria line and got himself a fried chicken plate with mash potatoes and green beans. He wanted the Mac and cheese, but that stuff didn't look like any Mac and cheese he'd ever eaten. Dam sat down and dug in. It wasn't too bad to be hospital food. He was getting ready to take another bite when Nurse Harris stopped at his table.

"Hello again, Mr. Shepherd."

He put his fork down. "Hello to you as well, Mrs. Harris."

"Do you mind if I sit down with you for a minute?"

He pointed to the chair on the opposite side of the table. "I'd love some company. Please join me."

"Thank you." She put her tray down on the table and sat down across from him. "And I'm not a Mrs. My name is Amarrea Harris, but most people call me Marri."

He extended his hand. "My name is Obadiah Damerae, but people call me Dam."

"Well Mr. Dam, first I want to apologize for the way I acted when you tried to help me the other day. I had no idea who you were, and my father had just given me the worst news."

"You were having a bad day. It happens."

"Still, I owe you an apology."

"Apology accepted."

They ate their food for a little while, then as Amarrea couldn't hold it in anymore, she said, "I've been thinking about what you did ever since y'all left your brothers room. And just so you know, he just now went to sleep. Before that, he kept clicking the nurse button and asking if I could come to his room. But each time I went into the room, all he did was ask for my number."

Dam chuckled. "That sounds like Dee. He is a complete mess, but we love him."

She looked over her shoulder to make sure none of her colleagues were in earshot. Turning back to Dam she said, "Can I be completely honest with you?"

"Of course, you can."

"The only reason the doctor told me to allow your parents in that room to see your brother was because we didn't think he was going to live much longer. We never allow more than two people at a time, but I felt awful about keeping you out of your brother's room especially since we thought he was dying."

"Knowing this makes me very thankful that you let me in his room. You could have lost your job if things had turned out differently."

"Tell me about it. I was scared out of my wits when he had another seizure right after I let y'all go into the room." She then leaned closer to Dam and whispered, "But here's the thing, this was his third seizure, and his vitals were failing. There was nothing more we could do for your brother. By all accounts, that third seizure should have killed him. But when I checked his vitals after that last seizure, his blood pressure and oxygen level was normal again. I just don't understand it."

Dam smiled at Amarrea. He was getting a funny feeling in his gut that this girl used to belong to the Lord and this was an opportunity to woo her back to Him. Don't let me mess this up, Lord. Dam asked her, "Do you believe in miracles."

"I've been trained to believe in science and medicine." She then shook her head. "But he never received that shot, yet his seizure stopped, now he's in that hospital bed acting as if nothing happened."

"I can explain it to you, if you care to listen," Dam told her.

"I interrupted your dinner, didn't I? Of course, I want to listen. I've got twenty more minutes on my break, so I'm all ears."

Just then, Dam was struck with the thought that God had Amarrea in the room when Dee received his miracle so that He could open her eyes to the truth. But what truth, was God trying to show her. Dam didn't know and didn't feel like it was his place to ask. His job was to deliver God's message and let the rest fall in place. "Do you read the Bible?"

She shook her head. "Not in a long time."

"I don't know if you've ever read the Gospels, but the story I want to tell you comes out of the book of Mark."

"The Gospels are Matthew, Mark, Luke, and John; right?"

He nodded. "I see you know a little something. Now let me tell you a story that just might clear things up. You see, during this moment in time, Jesus had been going throughout the land healing the sick and casting out demons. He had trained his disciples to do the same. But one day a man approached him, and said, 'Teacher, I brought You my son, who cannot speak and who has seizures that throw him down and cause him to foam at the mouth, gnash his teeth and become rigid. I spoke to your disciples and asked them to cast it out, but they could not.'"

"Based on your story, I'm guessing that the doctors and nurses are like the disciples that couldn't heal your brother, right?"

"You said that. I'm just trying to tell you a story."

"Carry on. Don't mind me, I just like asking questions."

"Anyway," he began again, "Jesus was basically saddened by the disciples, so he said, 'O faithless generation, how long shall I be with you? How long shall I bear with you? Bring him to Me.'

"They brought the boy to Jesus. And when the boy saw Jesus, immediately the spirit convulsed in him, and the boy fell on the ground and wallowed, foaming at the mouth. Jesus asked the father, 'How long has this been happening to him?' The father answered, 'From childhood. And often he has thrown him both into the fire and into the water to destroy him. But if You can do anything, have compassion on us and help us.'"

"Wait a minute." The nurse lifted a hand, halting the story. "So, you're telling me that this man's son had been dealing with seizures since he was a child and instead of taking the child to a doctor, they just waited on the day that Jesus would be walking through their town?"

"Bible doesn't say that the man never took his son to a doctor… maybe he did, maybe the doctors couldn't do anything to help, just as you all couldn't help my brother today." Dam waited for her to argue that fact, but when she said nothing, he asked, "Can I finish the story."

"Please, I'd like to hear the rest of this." Her lip slightly twisted in disbelief as she took a bite of her burger.

Dam didn't condemn her for the attitude she displayed. He understood all too well that many live with blinders on. It is up to the body of Christ to open blinded eyes. He continued with the story,

"After the man basically begged for help for his son, Jesus told him, 'If you can believe, all things are possible to him who believes.' Then the father of the child cried out and said with tears in his eyes, 'Lord, I believe; help my unbelief!'

"Then Jesus rebuked the unclean spirit, saying to it: 'Deaf and dumb spirit, I command you, come out of him.' The boy then stopped flopping on the floor and looked as if he was dead. Many of the people standing around even said that the boy was dead. But Jesus took the boy by the hand and lifted him up, and he arose." Dam took a deep breath before continuing the finale of the story.

"When the disciples saw this, they asked Jesus, 'Why could we not cast the demon out?' And Jesus told them, 'This kind of demon

71

can come out by nothing but prayer and fasting.' So, you see, Marri, the reason your medicine couldn't help my brother was because he needed a miracle from God. And I believe that you needed to see a miracle from God so that you can believe again."

Their eyes met and held for a long moment, then Marri looked away, glancing at the time on her phone. She wrapped up her sandwich and stood. "I've got to get back to my station. But thank you for telling me that story."

"I'm available anytime you want to talk. I mean that. If you have questions, don't hesitate to ask."

She stood there another moment, looking as if she wanted to say something, but by the time she opened her mouth, all she said was, "I'll keep that in mind."

He watched Marri walk away, understanding why his brother was trying to get close to her. Marri was indeed a beautiful woman. Dam had mostly dated women with long hair, but he had to admit that the short cut Marri was styling looked good on her. She had just enough hair for a man to run his hand through it and then be able to rest his hand on the nape of her long, slender neck.

Where did those thoughts come from? Why was he watching Marri walk away and day dreaming about running his hand through her hair? Dam didn't have time to be day dreaming like this. His brother was in trouble and Dam had to find some way to help him. He shook his head as he thought of his brother. Dee had always been a handful, so much so, that Dam could still remember the day and time that he first realized that his brother was a problem child. Dam was only three years old at the time, but he knew that his mother was not pleased with Dee's behavior...

His mom pulled up to the school to pick up Dee and Dontae. Dam was in the back in his car seat. His brothers opened the back door and climbed in. Neither one of them said hello or thanked his mom for picking them up.

"How was your day?" Mom asked Dee and Dontae as they jumped in the car.

"It was fun, Mama. I got first place in the math contest," Dontae said.

"You're just a regular math genius, aren't you?" Mama looked so proud of Dontae.

Dam tried to hug Dee as he got in the car, but Dee shoved his hand away, then flopped against the backseat and sulked.

Mama frowned as she asked, "What's wrong with you, Dee? Why are you being so mean to Dam?"

"Why did you have to bring him with you to pick us up? Daddy doesn't want him here, and neither do I."

"What a mean thing to say. Why on earth would you think that about your daddy?" Angel hoped and prayed that Demetrius hadn't told his sons how he feels about Dam.

"Don't pay him any attention Mama," Dontae said. "Dee is just mad because he got detention again today."

"Again?" This was the first Angel was hearing about any detention.

"Yeah, Mom. This is Dee's third detention this month. The teacher is threatening to suspend him."

For that bit of news, Dee reached over and punched Dontae in the arm. Dontae swung back, and Angel had to pull the car over to break the fight up. Then she had to spend a few minutes consoling Dam who was now crying as if he'd been punched. Once she settled Dam down, Angel pointed at Dee and said, "You're coming to church with me tonight. I think you need a little Jesus right about now."

"Daddy said I don't have to go to no dumb old church." Dee defiantly crossed his arm around his chest.

Since Dee was little, he had rebelled against the idea of so-called organized religion. He rarely attended church with the family once he was old enough to have a choice in the matter, and once he started working for Pop-Pop, Dee stopped showing up at church all together. All his years of rebellion had only brought him to this place... this space in time. And now Dam had to figure out how to help his wayward brother.

Dam threw his container in the trash can, put his tray on the shelf above the trash can and then left the cafeteria in search of his parents. He found them in the waiting area. As he walked into the area, he saw his mom's side profile as she sat in one of the chairs. She was leaning forward, talking to his dad.

Demetrius sat with his back towards the entrance, so he didn't see Dam come into the waiting area. But Dam heard every venomous word his father said about Pop-Pop. "When I left the business, I thought we were all finally free of my father and his way of doing things. I gave God's way a try, and I've been happy for it, Angel. I swear I have. But what Don has done to us, make me wish he wasn't my father and that I was still in the life. Because I would go to his hospital room right now and pop him. And then I'd stand there and watch him bleed out. That's what my family is used to doing to men who cross us."

"You talk like you hate your own father," Angel said as she placed a hand on her husband's arm, gently moving her hand from the top of his elbow to his hand as if that motion would calm the rage building in Demetrius Shepherd.

"I thought I had forgiven him for what he done to me all of my life… I mean this man was the cause of my mother getting herself killed when I was just a kid. But I prayed about all that I had against him, and I was truly making strides at forgiving that man." Tears rolled down Demetrius' face as he admitted, "Now I don't even know if I'll make it into heaven because I just can't forgive him this time. Not this time."

Dam was about to tell his father that he couldn't deny anyone forgiveness, especially since God had forgiven him for all the dirt he'd done in this life. But when he stepped into the area where his parents were sitting, looked at his father and saw the tears and pain on his face, Dam couldn't chastise his father.

He sat down next to Demetrius, put a hand on his father's back and just as his mother had been doing, he began to rub his back, trying to soothe away the pain. "Just remember, Dad, you got out. So, we can pull Dee out of the life too."

Demetrius lowered his head. He didn't say a word, but the tears continued to fall.

Right then, Dam understood that his father was just like that father who brought his son to Jesus asking that his son be healed from the demons that raged throughout his son's body. The body language Dam was seeing from his father was saying, 'Lord, I believe, but help my unbelief.'

8

Dontae, DeMarcus, and Dodi arrived at the hospital while they were still waiting to go back into Dee's room. Dontae had graduated college two years ago and was now working in Atlanta as a writer on church based drama that was leaving most of the Christianity out of its storyline.

DeMarcus had retired from football and was now having a very successful career as a sports analysis and commentator. Dodi was in her last year of high school, studying hard to keep her 4.0 GPA so she could be the first Shepherd family member to go to Harvard. Dam was proud of his brothers and sister, he recognized that God had blessed their family. Now they had to deal with the one who got away.

Later that evening Dee was moved to a regular room. The family still didn't want to overwhelm him, so they went in to see him two at a time. His mom and dad were first, then Dontae and DeMarcus. By the time he went in with Dodi, Dee had nodded off to sleep.

"Should we wake him?" Dodi asked as she leaned over the bed staring down at Dee.

"No, little sis. Dee needs to sleep. Let's just wait around to see how long it will take him to wake up."

"You have extra time on your hands since you just graduated from college. But I have an exam in the morning. I need to get back home to study."

"Then why did you wait until now to see Dee? You could have come in with one of the other brothers earlier, or even Mom and Dad."

Dodi came closer to Dam and whispered, "I'm mad at him. I don't know what to say to him. I'm not used to having a brother who is on drugs."

"I'm not on drugs, little miss princess. So, watch your mouth," Dee said, while he yawned and stretched out his arms.

Dodi turned to Dee with her hand over her mouth. "Sorry, big bro. I didn't know you could hear me."

"I was trying to sleep, but it's hard to do that when a brat is hovering all over you."

With her hands on her hips and anger in her voice, Dodi said, "I'm not a brat but what I want to know is why are you a drug addict?"

"Wow, you just slide right into it, huh?" Dam nudged his sister, trying to get her to chill.

"See, that's why I call you princess. Because you don't know nothing about these streets and what it takes to make it in this world."

"So, you need drugs to be a man and handle your business on the streets? Is that what you're telling us?" When he didn't answer, Dodi continued. "Daddy used to be in that life also. You are aware that all of us know this, right? He didn't become a drug head, and neither did Pop-Pop, so what's wrong with you?"

"Get out of here, Princess. Go home, study them books and mind your own business."

Looking at his sister, Dam could indeed see just how angry she was at Dee. All her life she had been catered and spoiled by all her brothers. She loved her brothers and wanted the best for us.

Dodi folded her arms across her chest, stumped her foot and huffed. "I'll leave. I've got better things to do than stand around and watch you kill yourself." With that, Dodi swung her Gucci purse onto her shoulder and stomped out of the room.

Dam sat down next to the bed. "Hey man, I'm sorry about that. Dodi doesn't mean any of what she said. She just doesn't like seeing you like this."

Dee looked toward the door that Dodi stumped out of. "I bought her that purse for Christmas. I've got half a mind to go through that girl's closet and take back everything I've bought that spoiled brat."

"I don't think Dodi is concerned about all the things you've bought her right now... she wants you to get better. Can't you see that?"

"Naw man, she's just being bratty. And I don't appreciate her talking to me like that."

"Dee, I'm not judging you, but come on, man. The way you live your life is a problem. You've got to make some changes, or this is not going to end well for you."

"And how would that be different from what life has already been like for him, huh?" Dee was defiant as he continued, "Do you know how hard it is being a Shepherd and trying to be on your own in them streets?"

"No, because I never tried to run the streets."

"Well I have, and I couldn't make any type of moves until I forced my way into Pop-Pop's organization. I thought he would be proud of me and let me take over, but he acts like I don't know what I'm doing and always send people to check behind me. Then I find out that he picked somebody else to run the business now that he's in the hospital... do you know how that made me feel?"

"Pop-Pop loves you, Dee. Maybe he finally realized that his life style is not right for his family."

Dee shook his head. "He just thinks I'm an idiot. All of y'all think I'm an idiot."

"Bro, why are you doing this to yourself. Your family loves you. We always have. We just don't understand why you can't straighten up."

"Yeah, Dad is always asking why I can't just do the right thing. But I think he has forgotten how many years I watched him do the wrong thing. I mean, wasn't he the head of our little crime family while Don was locked up?"

"So, all this time I thought I was doing the right thing by following in my father's footsteps, then I find out that my grandfather doesn't even trust me to run the business."

"Is that why you took that heroin?"

Dee leaned his head against his pillow and closed his eyes as if the light was bothering him. When he reopened them and looked at his brother, he admitted, "I just got tired of feeling like a failure. I just wanted to be numb and feel nothing."

Dam's heart went out to his brother. He'd always looked at him as the problem child of the family. Apparently, Dee felt the same way. But Dee hadn't been able to do anything about his reckless behavior. So, his brother thought sticking a needle in his arm would take the pain away. "How long have you been shooting up?"

A dark laugh escaped Dee's lips. "Believe it or not, I just started last week. Don always said that people who put that stuff in their bodies were fools and deserved whatever came to them. Now I know why he said that."

"What are you talking about?" Dam truly wasn't following.

"I know what Don has been doing? He acts so high and mighty. Like he's above all the other lowly drug dealers. But he's no better than anybody else. And his greed almost killed his grandson, just like we've been killing all those dumb addicts that drop dead with the needle in their arms every single day on these streets."

"What did Pop-Pop do?"

"Don't you get it... don't you know anything about these streets?" Dee rolled his eyes at his brother's ignorance.

Dam shook his head. "I don't know much about what's been going on. But educate me."

"Don cut the heroin with meth or something to give a faster high. That might sound like it's a good thing... but it's also a fast way to get dead. That's why so many addicts drop dead on the spot."

"You work for Pop-Pop. Didn't you know he was doing that... cutting the heroin or whatever?"

Dee shook his head. "He always told me the heroin wasn't cut. I never would have taken it if I thought it was."

"So, you did steal from Pop-Pop's stash?"

Dee shrugged. "I didn't consider it stealing. I am running the business with him... or at least I was... whatever."

Dee was truly hurt by the fact that Pop-Pop picked someone else to run his criminal empire. Dam was amazed by that. Why couldn't his brother see that what he and Pop-Pop was doing was wrong on so many levels? Dee had just admitted that the drugs they were putting on the street was killing people. Yet, he still wanted to run the business. Dam, lifted his head to the heavens, Lord, help me deal with this family of mine.

~~~~

As Angel and Demetrius walked through the parking lot on the way to their car, Angel tugged on Demetrius' arm. "Wait a minute, honey."

"Is something wrong?" He searched the parking lot, turning his head from one side to the other.

"Nurse Harris is sitting in her car."

"Who?"

"Dee's nurse." Angel pointed to the left. "She's crying. I need to talk to her."

"Okay, tell you what. I'm going back into the waiting area where I can at least sit down and watch the television."

"I know your game is about to come on, so I promise I won't be long."

"Yeah, yeah, yeah. You just better hope that I can turn this tv to ESPN." He smiled at her before walking away, letting her know that it was all good with him.

Angel silently prayed as she walked over to the car, "Lord, help me. Give me what to say to this young woman. She's hurting, and she needs You." Knocking on the passenger window, Angel waved at Nurse Harris and pointed toward the door.

Nurse Harris lifted her head off the steering wheel, leaned over and unlocked the door. She wiped her eyes as Angel sat down next to her.

Before saying a word, Angel pulled the young woman into her arms. And as she hugged her, she continued to silently pray. This girl was hurting, and for some reason, Angel felt as if she was at the exact place where God needed her to be. "It's going to be alright, Nurse Harris. Trust God."

"That's just it, I used to trust God with my whole life. But I stopped doing that years ago."

"Do you want to talk about it? I'm a good listener."

Amarrea laughed at that. "You're a good listener, and your son is the talker in the family I guess."

"Don't let Dee bother you. He has a lot of growing up to do."

Amarrea shook her head. "I wasn't talking about Dee... Dam and I talked during my lunch break. It's amazing to me how he has this unshakable faith in God."

"After all he has been through, sometimes I'm amazed by that fact. But it's true. Dam was born to serve the Lord, he has never wavered from that." Angel let silence penetrate the air for a beat or two and then she asked, "So, what's your story?"

Turning towards Angel, she sighed. "Where do I begin? Let's see… growing up I was in church all the time. I was a leader in youth group, a member of the praise and dance team. Oh yeah, and my father was the pastor of the church I attended. My mother was the first lady, I just thought we were a family blessed by God. That's what my father used to say all the time, 'Our family is blessed by God.' He told me that we had to appreciate all that God has done for us and love the Lord above all else. He preached righteous living, and I bought into all of it.

"But when I was sixteen, I came home from school one day and heard my mother in the bedroom crying and screaming at my father. I rarely listened at their door because I was a good girl and always did what was expected of me. But that day, I was drawn to that door, and as I stood there I couldn't believe what I was hearing…

"She was accusing him of cheating on her with some random women at our church. My father kept denying it, but my mother wasn't having it. She told him to take his clothes out of their bedroom. He moved into our guest room."

At that moment, Angel knew why God had her sitting in this car talking to this young woman. Nurse Harris could have been telling her very own story because she too was the child of a preacher who had cheated on his wife. Angel had been devastated, just as Nurse Harris had been.

"My father stayed in our guest room for two years, still standing behind that pulpit preaching like a man who loved God and lived what he preached. I prayed that he and my mom would fall in love again and stop acting like enemies in our home while pretending to be so loving when we were at church. But that didn't happen. When I turned eighteen and left for college. My dad moved out of the house, and they divorced before my freshman year was complete."

Angel wiped the tears from the woman's face as she told her, "I know how much you are hurting because the same thing happened in my family."

"Your father cheated on your mother too?"

Angel nodded. "My father was also a preacher. My mother divorced him and I pretty much divorced both of them, I ran away from home at the age of sixteen. I wanted nothing to do with either of them or the church for that matter."

"That's how I feel... or felt. I don't know. I'm confused right now. But I haven't been back to church since my first year in college. I've just been so disgusted with the whole thing. Too me, you can't trust these preachers. They stand behind those pulpits and lie."

Angel smiled for the first time during this conversation, not at Nurse Harris' indictment against the church, but because she believed she could help. "You and I, my dear are kindred spirits because I used to feel the same way."

Nurse Harris smiled a week smile. She realized that they had not been properly acquainted. "By the way I am Amarrea Harris, but most people call me Marri."

9

Before going home, Dam went back to his grandfather's hospital room. His father was dealing with an unforgiving heart because of all that Pop-Pop had done. Dam was beginning to feel some kind of way toward his grandfather. After hearing what Dad said about Pop-Pop causing the death of his mother and Dee saying that Pop-Pop cut the heroin he sold to make it more potent... not caring about whether people died from it, these were things that Dam couldn't get pass.

He and his grandfather had a great relationship. Dam had been praying for him since he was a child. But in all that time, he'd never imagined that his Pop-Pop was the reason he didn't have a grandmother on his father's side of the family.

"I didn't think I'd see you again today," Don said as he watched his grandson sit down in the lounge chair next to the bed.

"I need to talk to you, Pop-Pop. I know you're not feeling well, and I don't want to upset you, but..."

"We both know that I don't have much time left on this earth, so don't hold your tongue. Spit it out, and let's deal with it now."

He didn't like hearing his grandfather talk about death like it was right around the corner, but with how much damage he'd caused on this earth maybe it was best if he didn't live much longer. Dam immediately chastised himself as those awful thoughts crossed his mind. He didn't wish death on anyone, especially not his Pop-Pop. But he did need answers. "I heard Dad say something earlier that kind of shocked me because I'd never heard anyone in the family say this before."

Taking a deep breath, Dam just put it out there. "Why does dad think that you're responsible for his mother's death?"

Pain etched across Don's face and then quickly disappeared. "Nobody has brought this up to me in decades. Sometimes I trick myself into believing I forgot all about my beautiful Emma. But then she haunts me in my dreams, and I remember the whole horrible chain of events all over again."

"If this is going to be too much for you. We don't have to do this tonight."

Don waved a hand in the air, dismissing his grandson's comment. "I have a lot to atone for. I might as well start now."

A pain hit Don's body ripping through him, taking his breath away.

Dam stood and rushed to the bed. "You okay? Do you need me to get the nurse?"

When Don was able to speak again, he said, "Sit down grandson. I'm going to tell you this story. But I'm going to tell you even more than your father knows about what happened. Maybe one day you can tell him and ask him to forgive me for being too weak to say no to my own father.

"My old man was bigger than life and meaner than a rattle snake…and I thought he was the most powerful man on earth, even after my mother died from a drug overdose… my father had gotten her hooked on drugs… I still wanted to be just like him. I did whatever he told me because I was young and thought his way of doing things was the manly way. If I couldn't be like him, then I was a punk. And you couldn't be no punk around my daddy."

Don inhaled deeply. "Anyway, I was only twenty- three years old when I met Emma. She was eighteen and full of life, and prettier than any other girl in our neighborhood. Believe it or not, my Emma looks a lot like your mother, which is the reason I was so against the two of them getting together. But anyway, I fell for Emma instantly. She had my heart, and that's no lie. We eloped because my dad didn't want me marrying nobody."

"Why wouldn't your father be happy for you? That just seems crazy to me."

"Things were different back then. My father owned and operated a saloon and a whore house. He was well known for running women. He thought any man who couldn't control his woman was weak. So, when I got home and told him that I married Emma, he hit the roof. Told me I let some woman lead me around by the nose. He kept putting stuff in my head like Emma was running around on me. I told him it wasn't true, but he said, 'If she ain't running around now, trust me, she will be soon. It's in a woman's nature. They can't be trusted.'

"He kept putting those thoughts in my head, and then a couple of months after Emma had Demetrius she was hanging out with some friends, one of them was her old boyfriend. My father saw them and brought me over to the spot. I drug Emma away from her friends and refused to allow her to hang out with anybody. She was down for me, so Emma did what I said. Which was part of the problem."

Twisting his lip, like he didn't want the next few words to escape, Don said, "I owed my Dad money and couldn't pay him. That's when things turned really bad for Emma and me."

Dam watched his grandfather struggle with memories that were dancing in his head. He'd never in life seen this man shed one tear, but water fell from his eyes before he closed them so tight that nothing could get in, not even the past.

It looked to Dam as if his grandfather had fallen asleep. He was about to get up and leave so that Pop-Pop could get some rest, but just before he stood, Pop-Pop started talking again.

"I owed him money, and he wouldn't let it go... he was my father, so I thought he would let it go. But he waited until I spent six months in jail and then he got Emma hooked on drugs just like he got my mother hooked on drugs. By the time I got out of jail, she was already working for my father... my father," Don sounded like a wounded animal as he said, 'my father.'

"I wanted to kill my father. Instead, I moved me, and my family away and never spoke to him again. But the damage had already been done. Emma was a good mother, but she wasn't the wife I knew and loved any longer. We needed money to get me started in my own business, so I let her work the streets for me." He stopped abruptly and turned to Dam. "I never told your father any of this. Once I'm gone, do your Pop-Pop a favor and tell him that I never meant for his mother to get killed out on them streets.

"I let hatred of my father blind me to the fact that Emma needed my help. I can see it now, after all these year, but back then all I could see was that she had become a junkie just like my mother."

"But you loved her."

Don agreed. "I did. But I hated my father more. And I became every bit the hard and relentless man that my father had been. Those are the facts, Dam. It ain't pretty. I'm not a good man. I know that. But, all I want is for you all to know that somehow, I was able to break through the hardness in my heart and love all of you. Your dad might not believe that... but I loved him the only way I knew how."

"Don't you think it's time that you asked for forgiveness?"

Don shook his head. "I've done so much wrong in this world, I don't know who in their right mind would forgive me… just let your dad know that his mother was a good woman who's only fault was hooking up with a Shepherd."

"But Pop-Pop, you believe in God. I know you do. So, why won't you ask Him to forgive you? Why do you want to leave this earth like this?"

"You know why," Don told him as he closed his eyes and went to sleep. Dam stayed a little while longer. He kept looking at his grandfather wondering how this man who was so loving to him could be the same man that had let his wife turn tricks? When Dam finally got up, he slowly walked to his car wondering what in the world could be done for a man like his grandfather. Would Demetrius ever forgive him… would God ever forgive a man like The Don?

Driving down the street, Dam hit the steering wheel to take out his frustration. "Lord, I need Your help here. I'm telling my grandfather to ask for forgiveness, but I'm not even convinced that You would forgive a man like The Don. What am I supposed to do here, Lord? I just don't know."

Pop-Pop wasn't so hard that he didn't have regrets for some of the horrible things he'd done. But how was he ever going to convince his grandfather that those regrets and the burden of his sins could be lifted if he would just ask for forgiveness when he didn't believe it himself. Once again, part of the story he told Amarrea came back to mind, 'I believe Lord, but help my unbelief.'

Once he arrived at his parents' home, he went straight to his bedroom and climbed in bed. He was so drained from the events of the day that all he wanted to do was sleep and dream of sweet nothings. But that was not to be because the moment his head hit the pillow and his eyes closed, Dam was transported into a place where he had never been. It was hot, sticky and the smell took his breath away.

Coughing into his hand while simultaneously trying to keep the polluted, dry air out of his mouth, Dam gaged and felt like he was going to throw up. "What's going on?" This was like no dream or nightmare he had ever experienced. The walls around him were covered in slime that oozed down the wall like thick red blood.

A man stood next to Dam. He was clothed in vibrant and wondrous colors. Colors that were unlike anything Dam had ever seen. A hood hung over his head so Dam could not see his face. "Who are you?"

The man looked at him. "I am the Lord, the Christ that you serve."

Putting his hands up to his nostrils, Dam tried to block the gaseous and tainted air. "What's that smell?"

"It is the smell of decay, death, and dying."

"What kind of place is this? It doesn't feel like anything I've seen on earth."

"You're not on earth right now," Jesus told him as he stretched forth his arms. "This is a place where lost souls are tormented day and night. Come, let me show you."

They walked through a tunnel until they came to an opening. The very essence of evil sprang forth. Hundreds of menacing spirits stood, growling and snarling. The demons were of varied shapes and sizes. Some were as big as a grizzly bear with heads like bats and ten-inch fangs. Some were small and monkey-like, with big hairy arms. Still, others had large heads, large ears, and long jagged tails. The most dreadful of all were the smaller piranha-like imps. They infested their victims in swarms and gnawed at their flesh. The shadow of their leader swallowed the darkness as he towered over them. Green slime dripped from the tips of his flesh devouring fangs. He received his orders directly from Satan. It was his duty to loose these evil spirits on the inhabitants of hell and earth. He marched back and forth in front of his troops, hissing and drooling. His beady eyes glared at his troops one last time, then with a shout, commanded, "Go!"

The ominous beings flew up and out as the doors at the top of the belly of hell opened to spew these evil spirits out. Their captain continued shouting, "Destroy lives! Do evil! Confuse minds! Distort the truth! Go!"

Dam jumped back and grabbed hold of Jesus' arm as the remaining demons moved toward them.

"Fear not, Obadiah. They will not touch you. Not as long as you are with me."

"What's going on down here?"

"I will show you." Jesus then took him into an area of hell that housed numerous cages. "These cages are for those that relentlessly served Satan, and victimized others while they lived on earth."

Dam's skin scrawled as they entered the area. "Why do we have to come over here?"

"There is much you need to see here."

A man tightly gripped the bars of his cage and started screaming, "Help – help me, please. Come on, man. I know you hear me."

Dam fixed his eyes toward the noise, there was something familiar about the man inside that cage. And that voice... Dam stepped closer to the cage. "Who are you?"

"Help me, man. Get me out of here. I can't take it anymore."

Dam turned to Jesus. "Who is this man? He looks like my grandfather. Why does he look so much like Pop-Pop?"

"His name is Leon Shepherd. He is your grandfather's dad."

Dam swung back around to look at the man who had changed the course of all their lives. The man who had made his Pop-Pop a hardened criminal, and was in a way responsible for his own father not being able to forgive. It was a vicious cycle, Don hated Leon… Demetrius hated Don… and if this family didn't come together, Dee would soon hate Demetrius. And all of it began with this man, who was now suffering for everything he'd done.

"Don't just stand there. Do something to get me out of here."

Dam didn't want to help this man. Leon was right where he belonged. Thank God, he could do no further damage to their family.

Leon's eyes rolled back. He lifted his hand to his head and pulled at it as gut-wrenching screams escaped his mouth. But it wasn't Leon's mouth anymore. Leon was transforming into a deformed animal right in front of Dam.

The creature reached out. "H-help me!"

Dam jumped back. This was too much for him. "What's happening?"

Jesus touched Dam's shoulder. "While on earth he caused people to become things they were never meant to be. As punishment, his body now changes from one form to another. It will continue for eternity." He sadly shook His head and moved Dam away from the cells. "We have more to see."

Horrified, Dam had no wish to see more of this place, and he told Jesus so. Jesus kept walking.

"Where are we going now?" Dam inquired.

"To the Fun Room," Jesus informed him.

Dam doubted there was much fun in this awful place. He'd only been dealing with the heat and decay and the evil of this place for mere minutes, yet he didn't want to see anything else. He didn't even care what message the Lord was trying to deliver to him... deliver it another way, just let him go. How did these people stay in such a place for eternity?

The Fun Room had been created for those who once enjoyed the pleasures of sin and all its trappings. Dam held his nose as they walked into the room. *Smelled like a pile of trash had been dumped in this place.*

In this room, demons watched as tortured souls tried to recreate the fun they partook in on earth. Crap games were going on. Con artists recited their street hustle over and over again. Former CEOs and executives discussed business ventures.

They were permitted to do anything they wanted in the Fun Room, anything but leave. And that was the problem because there were also demons in the Fun Room. These demons taunted and tortured their souls. Every hour on the hour a bell would ring. The inhabitants of the Fun Room would tremble with fear and cry out for someone to save them. Dam wondered why these people had such a problem with a bell ringing; their bodies didn't change form or nothing horrifying like that. Then the demons grabbed a few unfortunate souls and brought them to the center of the room.

When Dam was a kid, he and Dontae had been kidnapped by a man name Todd. He was the security guards his father hired to watch over them. Dam had been terrified of Todd, but he was staring at him now as four demons marched around him like he was fresh meat. They hissed and cackled – spit and laughed. Now Todd was the one who was scared... real scared.

Initially, Dam wanted to cheer on the demons, like he was watching a football game and cheering for the opposing team. But then they started poking Todd with the long spears they carried. They pulled at his flesh. Todd let out a God-awful scream of agony that tore at Dam's heart.

Dam turned to Jesus "They're going to pull him apart."

"They often do."

"What do you mean?"

Jesus pointed to a pile of discarded limbs. "The demons enjoy mutilating these people. They will pick them apart until there is nothing left."

Dam looked back to the center of the room. Todd was crawling away from the demons. His right arm had been violently pulled from his body, but there was no blood. Dam watched as the demons brought another helpless man to the center of the room.

When the demons started in on their next victim, Dam questioned Jesus, "Why won't he run? Why don't you let these people defend themselves?"

"They made their choice," Jesus told him. His voice was sad but resigned. "Come."

"Why would anybody choose this?"

"They loved sin and committed sin until the day they died."

"But Lord, you can do anything. Can't you help them?"

"Come, I have more to show you." Jesus walked out of the Fun Room and headed toward a dark tunnel. Dam quickly ran to catch up with him. As they walked, Dam could hear more howling and cackling, and the cries of the lost souls. He came to a dead stop, mouth gaped open, as he pointed at a man crumpled and shaking in a corner. "He can't be here."

"For many years now."

"But he was a great minister of the Gospel. I studied his exploits in college."

"Even great ministers of the Gospel must serve the Lord in truth."

The tunnel ended, and the blackness of the great abyss gave way to pits of fire. Within those pits were souls. "These people once served the Lord, but they turned back to sin like a dog turns to his vomit."

They stopped in front of a battered and bruised woman. So much agony etched across her face that Dam was compelled to pray for her, even though he knew his prayers would go unanswered in this place.

Jesus then told him. "Her name is Emma Shepherd. She is your grandmother."

"No!" Dam screamed and turned his head away from the unbearable sight before him.

"She served me until she was eighteen years old. But the cares of the world turned her away."

Dam walked up to the pit that held the frame of his grandmother. Her shrilling cries of agony penetrated his heart. He bit his lip, trying to stop himself from screaming right with her. But as the flames from the fire licked at Emma's skeletal form, tears flowed down Dam's face.

Emma's decayed flesh hung by shreds from her bones. It burned and fell into the bottom of the pit. She had no hair left. It had long been burned from her skeletal frame. Her face was a hollow mass without eyes, just empty, neglected sockets.

When the flames died down, Dam could see the worms crawling through the bones of her skeleton. "Why do you torture her like this? Why can't you just forgive her? You said Yourself that she once served You," Dam cried.

"She never asked me to forgive her. She died before she could be restored back to Me."

The flesh crawled back onto her skeletal frame, and the fire started at her feet again. Small flames at first, but they grew, and climbed up her body. Fat and unrelenting tears flowed down Dam's face as he said, "I'm so sorry this is happening to you. Don wouldn't have wanted this for you, Grandma. He loved you, and his heart still aches for you."

When the flames subsided, and the worms were crawling up her body again, she turned to Dam. "Tell him to repent. Don't let him come to this place."

Dam turned wide eyes to Jesus. "Does she know who I'm talking about?"

Jesus nodded. "She knows who you are."

Excited at the thought that he could communicate with his grandmother, he hurriedly told her, "Your son, Demetrius hasn't forgotten you either." As he was talking to her, the flames licked at her bones again, and she screamed and screamed.

Dam wanted to dive into the pit and free his grandmother, but within a blink of an eye, Jesus had placed him in another space and time. Dam no longer felt the flames, no longer smelled that awful smell of death. "Where are we? Where is my grandmother?"

"There is someone else I would like for you to see."

"But I can't just leave my grandmother down there. Not like that, Lord, Please."

"I would have forgiven all her sins if she had asked. She did not, so there is nothing either of us can do for her."

10

Realizing that demons no longer swirled around him as they tortured misguided humans and that he wasn't watching fire lick at anyone's bones, Dam was relieved. But he didn't know where Jesus was taking him until he saw two angels standing outside the most magnificent pearl laden gates he'd ever seen. They opened the gates as they shouted, "Behold the Glory of God!"

"How is this happening, Lord. Am I actually witnessing heaven?"

"There's someone you need to meet."

As they walked through the pearly gates, Dam was awe struck as cushions of snowy white clouds caressed his feet. Instead of the smell of death and decay, his nostrils were greeted with a sweet flowery fragrant. As they continued to walk they came upon a great multitude of warrior angels. Their appearance was that of beauty and majesty. They wore radiant white garments with gold edge trim that embellished the front of the garment. At their waist, hung a huge golden sword, and large white wings flapped from behind.

"Where we are standing is the outer court of heaven. This is like a waiting room. The saints who served God on earth come here and wait to be admitted into the inner court and some, even go into the Holy of Holies. The warrior angels wait for their next assignments."

Dam was too awe struck to respond. He was amazed that he had been allowed to witness angels as they prepare to battle the monstrous demons that attacked us daily. He bowed down on one knee and yelled, "Glory to God in the Highest."

As he said those words, the captain of the angels handed out assignments and angels drifted away from the Outer Court, on the way to their assignment. They stood there for a moment watching as the most heavenly thing occurred, Jesus took him on the other side of the Outer Court.

If it was possible, this side was even more beautiful than the other. The tree of life stood bold and beautiful in the middle of the Outer Court. Its leaves were a heavenly green, and its fruit was succulent and enjoyed by all. Sweet blissful music could be heard throughout the great expanse of heaven. It was the harp, but it was better than any harp on earth; it was the guitar, but it was better than any guitar on earth.

There were thousands upon thousands of saints moving through the joys of heaven, clothed in glistening white robes, and bare feet.

Many had crowns on their heads with various types of jewels embedded in them. A woman stood, surrounded by the most beautiful array of flowers, colors without name. Heaven seemed like a great garden of love. Flowerbeds could be found all over this glorious place. As the woman stood in the midst of the splendor, Dam noticed that she had a crown on her head, but she only had one spot on her crown that appeared to be marked for a jewel, but the jewel was missing.

The woman glanced over at Dam and smiled. Then she lifted a hand and waved him toward her.

Turning to Jesus, Dam asked, "Why does she want me to come to her? Does she know who I am?"

Jesus nodded. "I told her I would bring you to see her?"

"Why didn't we just come here first? I like it here. But I don't ever want to go to that dark, evil place again."

"Imagine if the inhabitants of hell knew about the joys of heaven. They would give anything to make another choice as well. This is why we need your voice on earth. You will tell them not to go there... invite them to the glorious garden of heaven."

"But how, Lord? I can't even convince my own family."

The woman called to him again.

"Who is she, Lord?"

"She is your great grandmother. On earth, they called her Starlight."

Dam didn't hesitate. He swung back around and ran, tripping, falling… getting back up and running until he reached Starlight. She wrapped him in her arms, then laughed and laughed as she danced in the midst of the flower bed.

"I can't believe it. Are you truly my great grandmother?"

She nodded, smiled and continued twirling amongst the flowers.

He wanted to stop her. Ask her to sit down and talk to him. How he would love to know how she was able to get to heaven when the others did not. But Starlight had forgotten about him and was now rejoicing and praising God, just as all the other inhabitants of this wondrous place were doing. He stepped out of the garden of flowers and made his way back to Jesus.

"She didn't want to talk," Dam felt a bit dejected.

"The inhabitants of heaven spend most of their time praising God for His goodness to them. Starlight knows that you are a servant of God and she is praising God for that."

Confusion etched on Dam's face as he asked, "How did she get here? Don't get me wrong. I'm thankful, but from the life, my grandfather told me she lived, I would have expected to see her in that dark, evil place we just left."

The Lord answered by saying, "Dam, do you know that you were predestined from your mother's womb to serve the Lord?"

Now it was Dam's turn to smile. "I've been told that a time or two or three."

Jesus then pointed toward Starlight. "She is the reason."

"I don't understand."

With a wave of a hand, Jesus took them out of the Outer Court and into a dark room. Dam was about to freak out, thinking that Jesus had taken him back to hell, a place he never wanted to see again. Matter-of-fact, he never wanted anyone else to see that place either. He had to do something to help his family.

Against the black wall in front of them, a scene began playing out as if they were in a theater room watching a movie. But this was like no movie he'd ever seen. For one thing, the world-renowned preacher Dam had seen in hell was in a bedroom putting his clothes on while Starlight laid in the bed looking up at him. The look on her face indicated she didn't seem to like this man very much.

"You on your way back to church?" She asked in a sneering tone.

He swung around, nostrils flaring. "I told you not to mention the church to me."

"Why can't I mention the church or even God to you." She put her nightgown on then got out of the bed and strutted over to him. "Am I not good enough for your God? Does He not love me just as much as He loves you? You do know that we are both sinners, right? It's not just me."

He slapped her so hard that she fell down. Blood trickled from her lip as he loomed over her with cutting words. "I am not a sinner like you. I serve the Lord faithfully. I may have weak moments in which

I stumble, but I have done so much for the kingdom of God that all I have to do is ask for forgiveness and He will forgive me."

"Won't He forgive me too," Starlight screamed back at him as he was about to hit her again.

The preacher stepped back as if he'd been pushed away from Starlight. He ran his hand through his hair. After, taking a few deep breaths to settle himself, he said, "The whore Mary Magdalene was forgiven by Jesus, so I guess you too could absolve yourself of such filthy and unredeemable character." He stepped over her and swung the door open.

"Wait," Starlight shouted.

"I put your money on the dresser."

"I don't care about that." Starlight stood up. "I need to know how to get this forgiveness from your God. I want to see my son again, but he won't have anything to do with me unless he knows I've changed."

The preacher closed the door and stepped back into the room. He had a look of compassion on his face as he told her, "Forget what I said earlier. I was just angry because you compared yourself to me… now listen to what I'm about to tell you."

Starlight sat down on the edge of her bed, but she kept her eyes on the preacher and listened to every word he said.

"If in your heart, you are ever truly sorry for the way you've lived and want Jesus to take away your sins, you just have to ask the Lord to forgive you and ask Him to come into your heart and save you. Okay?"

As the scene ended, Dam turned to Jesus. "If that preacher understood about forgiveness, why didn't he go to heaven when he died?"

"Because his heart had been hardened."

"So, you're telling me, that even after all Starlight been through, her heart had not been hardened to the truth of God's forgiveness?"

"See for yourself."

Dam was now viewing another sad scene staring his great grandmother. But in this scene, she was high, his grandfather was yelling at her and saying hateful things to her.

Dam told Jesus, "He didn't mean it. My grandfather loved his mother. He just hated what she became."

"Starlight knew that… keep watching."

When Dam turned back, his grandfather was no longer in the room berating Starlight. But she didn't look good like she had lost all hope in life. She was on a bathroom floor with a needle in her arm, her eyes closed, head kicked back as the juice flowed through her veins. She jumped, eyes bucked. She grabbed hold of her heart.

Starlight slumped over and then she lifted a hand to heaven as she said, "Forgive me, God. Save my soul so I can hold my son in my arms one more time." Starlight then flopped to the ground and went still.

"Is she dead? Please tell me I didn't just witness Starlight's death."

"What you just witnessed was Starlight receiving forgiveness from God and entering into her eternal rest."

After those words from Jesus, Dam's eyes opened, and he was back in his bed. Looking around the room as if he expected to see someone else in there with him. But when he found no one else, he sat up and ran a hand over his face. "What just happened? And what am I supposed to do about it?"

As he laid there trying to wrap his mind around what he'd witnessed as he traveled through the spiritual realm with his Lord and Savior, Dam started putting it all together. He lifted his Bible from the end table next to his bed and turned to the thirteenth chapter of Luke.

His prayer partner had quoted the story of the fig tree from this chapter just the other day, but if Dam remembered correctly; the beginning verses of that chapter were just as important for what he was going through. He began reading at the first verse:

There were present at that season some who told Jesus about the Galileans whose blood Pilate had mingled with their sacrifices. And Jesus answered and said to them, "Do you suppose that these Galileans were worse sinners than all other Galileans because they suffered such things? I tell you, no; but unless you repent, you will all likewise perish. Or those eighteen on whom the tower in Siloam fell and killed them, do you think that they were worse sinners than all other men who dwelt in Jerusalem? I tell you, no; but unless you repent, you will all likewise perish."

"Jesus, thank You," Dam shouted as he threw back the cover and jumped out of bed. He knew what needed to be done now.

11

Dam had ear buds in his ears jamming to praise music as he entered the hospital. He was so caught up listening to *This Means War* by Pastor Charles Jenkins that he didn't see Amarrea rushing over to him.

Poking his arm to get his attention, Amarrea said, "You seem in good spirits today."

Taking the ear buds out, Dam said, "This is the day the Lord has made, I shall rejoice and be glad in it."

Amarrea smiled. "You and your mother have a way about you. When I'm around either of you, it makes me believe that God really does care. How do y'all do that?"

"Because it's true and we believe it, simple as that."

"You make it sound simple, but it's really not that simple," Amarrea told him, but then quickly changed the subject. "I saw you walking in, so I thought you'd want to know that we are getting ready to release your brother."

"Do my parents know?"

"They're in the room with him right now. I'm assuming they'll be driving him home."

"That's good. I need to talk to my grandfather. So, I'll try to get to Dee's room before he's released, if not, I'll catch up with him later."

"I don't want to hold you up. Just wanted to let you know about your brother."

Dam realized that he was just standing there staring at Amarrea, even after he'd told her he needed to talk to his grandfather. His feet seemed stuck in that spot... it was like his body wanted to be where Amarrea was. But he was on an assignment so he would have to check that at another time and figure out why he was having feelings for Amarrea once he took care of God's business. "Okay... then. I guess I'll see you later."

"Later." She waved at him as she walked away, leaving him standing at the entrance of the hospital.

Dam regaining his footing and headed for the elevators. He didn't understand why that woman left him feeling out of sorts at every meeting, but he had to stay focused. Dam was determined that Pop-Pop would listen to him today. God had delivered a message to Dam last night that was so clear that even his grandfather wouldn't be able to miss what it meant.

But when he walked into the hospital room he found his grandfather in the bed with hand and leg restraints. There was a bandage on his head and several bandages on both arms. He rushed to the nurse's station. "What happened to my grandfather? Why did you restrain him like that?" Dam was yelling at the nurse behind the desk as he pointed toward his grandfather's room.

"I called your father early this morning and left a message," the nurse said as she stood up and followed Dam back to the room. "When I did my rounds, Mr. Shepherd was thrashing all over the bed, blood was gushing from a gash on his head, and there were cuts on his arm."

"Did someone attack him? Don't you have security in this hospital?"

"No one else was in the room. I promise you, I witnessed your grandfather attacking himself. I don't know what's going on because I couldn't wake him up. I thought it best to restrain his movement until we can wake him up."

Confusion danced across Dam's eyes. "Wake him up? What do you mean, he won't wake up? Is he in a comma or something?"

"We don't know yet. We're waiting on the doctor to get here so tests can be ran."

Dam stood over Don's bed. He shook him. "Wake up Pop-Pop, I really need to talk to you."

~~~~

Don was in the battle of his life and couldn't open his eyes, even though he desperately wanted to. He could hear Dam talking to him, but he was busy fighting off this big, monstrous demon who was trying to keep him locked down in hell.

Don wasn't going out like that. He'd been knocked down and poked and kicked, but he kept getting back up. But as soon as he got up another demon with sharp tentacles and bat like wings, swooped down on him. That demon clawed at Don's face while another gut punched him so hard he flew into a black slimy wall, then fell to the ground again.

"Don't get back up, Don. You can't win down here."

As Don laid on the ground winded and trying to figure a way out of the predicament, he was in; he heard a voice he hadn't heard in twenty years. Was he hallucinating? Had the blows to the head he received affected him so bad that he was imagining things?

"It's me, Don."

Don lifted his head and was greeted with the cowering presence of Stan Michael. Stan had been Don's, right-hand man. They had broken bread together, fought many battles and served prison stints together… and never in any of that time had he seen Stan cower or even give the appearance that he was scared of anything. But he was scared now. "Am I dreaming, man? What are we doing in a place like this?"

Stan lowered his head and shook it. "If you're down here with me, probably dead."

"Dead? I'm not dead."

"Then how are you talking to me? I've been dead for many years now."

"I know. I remember you dying." Don glanced around the dark and gloomy room. When he didn't see another demon waiting to attack him, he stood and walked over to Stan. "Is it really you, man?" He reached out to touch Stan.

But Stan jumped, moving away from Don's hand. "Every bone in my body aches. I don't like to be touched."

"Have these demons been attacking you too? Yo, look, we've got to get a crew down here so we can strike back. Don't nobody mess with us like this and get away with it."

"I thought the same thing when I first came here. To me, this place was just like prison, with no way out. But it's worse than any prison we've ever seen or heard of, 'cause these demons don't play. They get off on torturing us. And the torture never ends."

"Come on, Stan. We don' been through too much for you to punk out now."

"You don't know what it's like down here, and how I wish you never would have found out. I wouldn't wish this place on my worst enemy."

"I get it. It's a pit down here. The smell is the worst thing to me. The heat mixed with the smell of death makes me want to throw up."

"You get used to the smell," Stan told him. "But you never get used to…" a bell chimed, and Stan started shaking and looking for a place to hide.

Before Don could figure out why something that sounded more like a school bell ringing would incite such fear three demons surrounded him, Don understood clearly what the problem was. It was feeding time. "Get away from me."

"Don't say anything," Stan shouted. "It'll go easier for you if you just shut up."

One of the demons picked Don up and twirled him around like he was a human billboard. Don was then body slammed onto a bed of fire. He heard his body sizzle from the heat that scorched through to his body. Don wasn't talking back, he was screaming. He screamed until he passed out.

"Oh, thank You, God." Dam said as his body burned through and through. The torture would be over soon because there would be nothing left of him.

One of the demons pulled him out of the fire and shoved a knife through his chest. "There's no God here, you idiot. Don't you know where you are?"

~~~

"He's flatlining!"

Dam heard the words and then witnessed a swarm of activity around his grandfather. He was holding onto Don's hand, yelling into

117

his ear, "Don't die, Pop-Pop. Not yet. I have a message from Starlight."

They pushed Dam out of the way as they put the defibrillator to Don's chest. They had to send those currents through his body twice before the lines on the monitor created those hills and valleys again. Dam exhaled, not even realizing that he had been holding his breath.

Don groaned. His head flop from one side to the other as he mumbled, "I deserve this. I deserve it."

Dam's eyes widened as he heard his grandfather say those words. He now understood what had happened to him. Don had visited hell, and he discovered that he wasn't about to win any fights down there. God had shown Pop-Pop what becomes of thugs who think they're so hard that they don't need Him. Now all Dam had to do was convince Pop-Pop to accept the Lord as his savior.

Since Don was not thrashing around in the bed or trying to hurt himself anymore, they took the restraints off his arms and legs. Dam then had an idea. He called the hospital operator. When she answered, he said, "Can I get the nurse's station for Demetrius Shepherd Jr's room."

"One moment please."

The operator connected him. As the phone was answered, Dam said, "Can I please speak to Nurse Harris."

"One moment." The line went silent and then...

"How can I help you?"

"Amarrea, is that you?"

"Yes, who am I speaking with?"

"This is Dam. Have you released Dee yet?"

"I just picked up the wheelchair. I'm getting ready to take him to the car."

"I need a huge favor from you."

~~~~

"Why are we getting off the elevator on the third floor?" Demetrius asked as the elevator door opened and Amarrea pushed Dee's wheelchair out.

"We need to get something on this floor before you can leave," she explained.

Angel and Demetrius stepped out. Angel said, "As long as we're on this floor, why don't we check on Don before leaving?"

Demetrius kept walking towards Don's room, but his protest could be heard throughout the corridor. "I don't see why we have to check on him. Dam is with him, that should be good enough for the old man."

"Mighty Christian of you, Dad," Dee said from the wheelchair as Amarrea continued pushing him down the hallway.

"Tell you what, Son. I'll worry about my Christianity while you worry about your drug abuse."

"Demetrius!" Angel glared at her husband. "That wasn't called for."

Demetrius stopped walking. He lowered his head a bit. "Wait a minute." Angel and Amarrea stopped with him.

"I was wrong for what I just said, Dee. I hope you can forgive me." He turned to Angel. "I'm sorry for how I've been acting lately, but you've got to understand where I'm coming from. My father is poison. He has done so much damage to our family." Demetrius sighed. "It's hardened my heart Angel, and I'm praying to God for a change. But it's just not in me yet."

"You can do this Dad." Dam said as he stepped outside of Don's room, which was just two doors down from where they were standing. "You're not the only one whose heart has been hardened by the actions of his father. The same thing happened to Pop-Pop. I'll tell you everything he told me if you would just come into his room."

When Demetrius didn't respond. Dam said, "Come on, Dad. I know you want to help. Your father doesn't have much time left. I just watched them use a defibrillator on him after he basically flatlined. This may be our last chance to get Don Shepherd, the notorious gangster who caused much fear and trembling in his day to believe that he can be forgiven. Because he'll be the one in fear and trembling if he doesn't make it into heaven."

"He doesn't need me. He needs to ask the Lord to forgive him for all the harm he's done."

"Just like the Lord forgave you, huh, Dad?" Dee smirked, a look of contempt on his face as he looked at his father.

"He won't ask for forgiveness because he doesn't think he deserves it," Dam told Demetrius.

"You can stay out here if you want to, but I'm going in there," Angel told her husband.

"Me too, Ma." Amarrea pushed Dee's chair forward, they entered Don's room.

Angel was right behind them. When she entered, Don's head slightly lifted off the bed. "Emma, don't tell me you're down here too. I'm so sorry honey. I never would have wanted this for you."

12

Demetrius heard his father call Angel by his mother's name and rushed over to the door behind Dam. "What is he talking about?"

"He thinks mom is Emma. He told me that Mom resembles her."

"I don't care what he thinks. He shouldn't have my mother's name in his mouth after what he did. He shouldn't even have Angel's name in his mouth for that matter. Because he caused her a lot of pain too."

"And Mom forgave him, Dad. Don't you think it's time you freed yourself too?"

Demetrius shoulders slumped in defeat. He wanted to be free of this hate that was dogging him. But his father had been hurting him all his life, and he'd accepted it. Then his actions cause his wife to be raped. That happened a long time ago, so Demetrius tried to get over that, especially since his wife had forgiven his dad. But then Don took Dee under his wing in his illegal business and Demetrius was done.

"This is so hard for me, Dam. Your grandfather has done too much to me and mine... and now I'm supposed to just forget about all of that."

Dam moved his father away from the entrance to Don's room. There was a small waiting area with six chairs and a television not far from the nurse's station. He took his father there and sat down with him. "Dad look, I know you may not believe this, but Pop-Pop loved Grandma Emma. It broke his heart when she died."

"Then why did he have her turning tricks for him in the first place? That's not love. I never would have asked your mother to do anything like that."

"His father caused a lot of problems for Pop-Pop and Emma."

"Sounds familiar. Just like that old man caused problems for Angel and me," Demetrius said bitterly.

"It was his father who got Emma on drugs and started her turning tricks. You don't know the story, but Pop-Pop told it to me last night. He wanted you to know what happened back then and he wanted you to forgive him for how he allowed his heart to be hardened towards Emma."

"Don has never mentioned his dad to me. I didn't even think I had a grandfather until I heard some of his boys whispering about the man's death. They were actually debating whether or not to tell Don."

"That's because Pop-Pop hated his father, probably even more than you hate him."

"I don't hate Don... I just don't want anything to do with him," Demetrius corrected.

"It wasn't Pop-Pop. His father was a very unforgiving man, when Don went to prison, he still owed Leon some money. Instead of your grandfather taking care of you and grandma while Pop-Pop was away, Leon got her hooked-on drugs and then turned her out, so she could pay off Pop-Pop's debt.

"When he got out of prison he took you and Emma as far away from Leon as he could get. But Emma was hooked on drugs by that time and Don's heart had hardened not only for his father but for her as well."

Demetrius stared at his son, eyes filling with unshed tears. "He never told me any of this."

Dam put a hand on Demetrius' shoulder. "He asked me to tell you, Dad. He needs you to forgive him. There's been too many hard hearts in this family... free yourself and let's cut this curse of hate from the root."

~~~~

As Demetrius and Dam walked into Don's room Angel was standing by the bed. She was crying as she told Don, "I don't blame you, Don. Be at peace, knowing that I forgive you."

Don shook his head. "We'll never be at peace down here, Emma. Go, hide yourself before the demons come back to get us."

"What is he talking about?" Demetrius asked.

Dee shrugged as he told him. "I don't know what happened to him, but Pop-Pop thinks he's in hell. And he thinks that his wife is there with him."

"You don't have to stay in hell, Don. You still have a chance to go to heaven. Can I pray for you?" Angel was still crying, but she was determined to recite the sinner's prayer with Don before it was too late.

"No, I deserve this. I ruin everything I touch, Emma. I even ruined our son's life. I'm getting what I deserve, but I never wanted this for you."

Dam whispered to his father. "Is your life in ruins? Or has God blessed you with a beautiful wife, kids and a legal business that affords you a very good living."

With that said, Demetrius finally saw what God had been trying to show him all along. Don didn't control his destiny anymore. God was his heavenly Father, He had turned Demetrius' life around. God had forgiven Demetrius for all his wrong. It was time for him to free his father.

Demetrius stepped to the other side of the bed. "My life is not in ruins, Dad. God has been good to my family and me, He wants to be good to you too."

Don's eyes filled with terror and he wept. "Demetrius, dear God, please tell me you're not in this God forsaken place with us."

"Stop crying Dad." Demetrius had never seen his father shed a tear over anything. The hardness in his own heart cracked as he witnessed this. "I'm not dead, and neither are you. You're still in the hospital."

Don calmed down a bit as he confirmed with his son. "You're not in hell?"

"No Daddy, when I die, I will be in heaven, and we want you to go there to. I forgive you for everything Dad. Can you please accept the Lord into your heart and ask Him to forgive you, so that you and I can be in heaven together one day?"

Don closed his eyes as he meditated on Demetrius' words. When he opened his eyes again, he admitted, "I don't want to go back there... but it's not fair for me to go to heaven, is it, Son?"

Dam stepped up, to the foot of the bed. "Listen to me Pop-Pop. I know what you experienced because God allowed me to see both heaven and hell last night. And I came here this morning to tell you who I met in heaven."

Don's eyes started closing, he was getting weak again. He felt like going to sleep... he was so tired, Don didn't know if he'd wake from this sleep.

"I saw Starlight. She was happy and dancing... and waiting on you."

"Starlight," he mumbled as he drifted.

"Shake him a little, Dad," Dam said to his father. He then kept talking to Don. "Starlight asked the Lord to forgive her for everything she did. And God forgave her. Lift your hands, Pop-Pop and accept God's love."

"Starlight," he mumbled again.

"Come on, Don, do it for Emma. She doesn't want to see you down there. You wouldn't be able to help her anyway," Angel told him.

"No, I wouldn't be able to help. I couldn't help Emma."

"Help yourself, Pop-Pop. Repeat after me... Lord Jesus, I am a sinner, I need You to forgive me."

Don's hands slowly lifted. "Lord Jesus, I am a sinner, I need You to forgive me."

"Come into my heart, Lord and make me brand new," Dam continued.

"Come into my heart, Lord and make me brand new..." Suddenly, Don's hands flopped as he went still. The monitor went crazy beeping as Don flatlined again.

13

Demetrius laid on Don's chest and let the tears fall. He and Don had a love/hate relationship for most of his life, but after hearing about what Don went through with his own father, Demetrius finally had compassion for his dad. Now it was over, and he was left feeling as if he'd wasted too much time being angry when he could have spent those final days forgiving and loving his father. "What have I done?" He kept asking as he continued to lay his head on his father's chest. "What have I done?"

Angel put a hand on Demetrius' back and tried to soothe away his pain. "It's okay baby. Don is in a better place now. And it's all because of you. He never would have accepted Christ if you hadn't forgiven him. Just remember that."

Slowly, Demetrius lifted his head and moved away from Don's lifeless body. He was about to put his arms around Angel because he was so grateful for her comfort. But then he noticed that Dee had his head in his hand, crying uncontrollably. Dam was crying too, but it was a different kind of cry. Dam's hands were lifted, and he was rejoicing.

Demetrius knew then this was no time for him to feel sorry for himself about the time he missed with his father. It was a time of great joy because God had been gracious to another member of the Shepherd family.

Demetrius walked over to Dee and bent down in front of him. "I know you're going to miss Pop-Pop. I'm going to miss him too. But we should be rejoicing because he just entered into Paradise."

As he tried to wipe the tears from his face, Dee blubbered, "I never thought he would do it. Gangsters don't go out like that. We're supposed to be hard to the end."

"Is that how you see it. You think my father was weak for accepting the Lord at the end of his life?"

"I don't know... Yeah, something like that. I guess." Dee was so confused right now he didn't know what was right.

Dam started laughing at him. "Boy, don't you know that gangsters don't run nothing in hell. They are tormented night and day just like everyone else who goes down there."

"No one is talking about going to hell, little bro."

Dam was so thankful to His Lord and Savior for allowing him to see the truth for himself. The knowledge he now possessed would help him set his brother straight. "People don't get a choice in where they will spend eternity. The choice you get is whether or not to believe that Jesus Christ came to save all of us from our sins. And then you have to decide whether or not to ask God to forgive you for sins you've committed."

Dam then pointed toward Don. "You don't get to disparage Pop-Pop because he finally made the best decision of his life and now, because of it, he will spend eternity in heaven. And I pray that God allows me to see him again when it is my time. What about you, bro?"

Dee didn't respond. He fixed his eyes on his grandfather's lifeless body. He then shook his head, got out of the wheelchair and walked out of the room.

"Don't just leave, Dee. Talk to us," Angel took a step, getting ready to follow her son.

But Demetrius stopped her. "Let him go, hon. He needs time to think."

"But... I," Angel struggled with her thought.

"Trust God, hon. We just witnessed a miracle with my dad. Don't you think God can do the same with Dee?"

~~~~~

As they all walked out of Don's room, Amarrea pulled Dam to the side. "I am so sorry about your grandfather, and I know that you need to be with your family right now. But I was wondering if I could talk to you when I get off work tonight?"

Dam gave her his telephone number and the address to the house. "Come by when you get off. I'll be there."

Amarrea was a mess after the Shepherd family left the hospital. She kept going back and forth into the bathroom as her emotions took over. She took a patient's blood pressure and then she thought about everything that happened with the Shepherd family, sending her on an emotional roller coaster, she was a wreck. Amarrea rushed to the bathroom, closed herself behind a stall and cried until she couldn't cry anymore. She went back to work only to find herself having to repeat the entire episode all over again when her emotions got the best of her. This went on for the remainder of her shift.

She had never been so happy for her work day to end as she was today. It had been an emotionally exhausting day, but she was looking forward to seeing Dam. This thought seemed to give her a burst of new energy. Amarrea jumped in her car, put Dam's address in her GPS and drove straight to his house without stopping to pick up anything to eat, even though she had skipped lunch earlier. She had spent her entire break in the bathroom stall. The hunger pains were beginning to rumble in her stomach.

When she reached Dam's place, she wasn't hardly embarrassed to accept the plate of food Angel offered her. Amarrea was enjoying the moment and her food as she and Dam sat on the back patio eating fried chicken, Mac & cheese, and green beans. "This is so good, I'm not even going to think about what it's doing to my arteries."

Dam agreed with her and said, "Word got around about Pop-Pop, and people started bringing all kinds of food over. I've been eating all day."

"This is my first meal since my smoothie at breakfast." Amarrea's mouth was full of food as she tried to talk.

"I can tell," Dam said, laughing at her.

"Okay, well give me a minute." Amarrea then took another bite of her chicken. She ate every piece of food on her plate and then leaned back against the cushion of the oversized chair she was sitting in and exhaled.

"Feel better?"

She nodded. It was amazing to Amarrea, but she always felt better when she was around Dam. He made her feel safe and cared for. He opened her eyes to the possibility of God's love in ways she hadn't considered since she was sixteen years old. "Seems like I've been crying since I met you. But today, I think my tears were cleansing for me."

Dam was sitting across from Amarrea. He patted the seat next to him. "Come sit next to me."

Amarrea did as he requested. Dam put his arms around her and pulled her close. He then whispered in her ear. "Whatever you're dealing with... just trust God."

She leaned back and looked into Dam's eyes. He had beautiful eyes. Everything about this man was beautiful to Amarrea. He made her believe again, she would never forget that. "My father is a preacher. He cheated on my mother for years, and now he's marrying the woman he cheated on my mom with."

"Wow, I didn't see that one coming."

"Me either. Growing up, I idolized my dad. I believed he was a true man of God. But his actions destroyed my faith. And that's why I didn't think much of you when we met."

"And I told you that I was a minister," Dam finished.

"I wasn't trying to hear that," Amarrea admitted. "So-called men of God were scumbags as far as I was concerned… but then you opened my eyes to God's healing power and the power of forgiveness, suddenly I believe again."

"Then why do you look so sad, Amarrea Harris?"

Sighing deeply and then leaning back against Dam's strong shoulder, she said, "I'm struggling with forgiving my father."

"It takes some people a long time to get over hurt. Look at my father today. He and my grandfather hadn't spoken to each other in years. Now that Pop-Pop is gone, my dad regrets all the time he spent being angry and stubborn."

"I saw that. And that's why I've been crying all day long. Even after everything he's done, I still love my dad and I don't want to wait until he's dying before I forgive him."

"Then what's the problem?"

"It's easier said than done I guess. That man hurt my mother, and he hurt me."

"My grandfather hurt a lot of people, but God was still willing to forgive him. We can't deny others forgiveness when God doesn't deny us."

"Would you pray for me?" Amarrea asked.

Dam took her by the hand and prayed. When he was finished, he told her, "God loves you, Amarrea. And He wants you to be free of the pain you're carrying around."

"Thank you, Dam." She leaned forward and kissed him. Her eyes widened, and she hopped off the sofa. "I'm sorry. I shouldn't have done that."

Dam shrugged. "I didn't mind, so if you want to do it again…" he let his words hang out there.

"I'd better go." Amarrea made her way back into the house and said her goodbyes to everyone.

Angel hugged Amarrea and then hugged Dam so she could whisper in his ear. "She's the one, Son. Don't let her get away."

Dam walked Amarrea to her car and opened the driver side door. As she took her seat, he leaned down and kissed her on the forehead. "Be safe, beautiful."

Smiling up at him, Amarrea felt butterflies from down deep in her soul. She put her hand over her stomach. "I'll see you later."

"Alright, Ms. Amarrea." He stepped away from the car and watched her back out of the driveway. She waved at him and then drove down the street. But somehow, Dam didn't feel like this was goodbye.

~~~~

Dam was proud to do the eulogy at his grandfather's homegoing service. It was a time for celebration because a saint was marching into heaven. He hadn't been a saint all his life, he'd prayed for forgiveness just in the nick of time. But this race is not given to the swift, neither to the strong but to he that endures until the end… and Dam liked to think, even to he that asked for forgiveness in the end.

However, as he preached the homegoing message, he told everyone in attendance about how his grandfather finally accepted God into his life. But he admonished them not to wait until the last minute to accept the forgiveness that God freely offered. "Don't let it be said, too late."

At the end of the eulogy, Dam gave an altar call. He smiled as he viewed all the old-head gangsters and some young ones too, standing at the altar crying out to God. But what really got him was when he watched Dee, and Al walk down the aisle and lift their hands, accepting Jesus as their savior.

Dam was thanking the Lord for his grandfather's old friend accepting Christ and for Dee finally giving God a try. And it was at that moment he realized that he wouldn't be able to take that youth pastor job. God was moving him toward another assignment and Dam was ready to accept whatever God had for him.

He didn't think the day could get any better and he knew that his Pop-Pop was smiling down at them from heaven. But then something happened that put the icing on the cake. When the funeral was over, and Dam was driving to his parent's home for the repass, Amarrea called him.

"I wish I could have been there with your family today," she told him, "but my father's wedding was today, and I had to attend."

"Were you finally able to forgive him?"

"That's why I called you. I wanted to thank you for coming into my life when I really needed someone to tell me the truth."

"Glad I could help."

"Can I take you to dinner to show my appreciation? I'd offer to cook for you, but my family says that I'm more of an ook, than a cook."

Dam busted out laughing. "Alright, Ms. Amarrea. You don't have to cook for me. And you don't have to take me to dinner. Because I want to take you to dinner. I really want to get to know you… can you handle that?"

"I think I'd like that very much."

They made arrangements for their date and then hung up. Dam was excited because, just as his mother had said, Amarrea was the one for him. He had his ministry and his lady, what more could one man ask for? "Thank You, Lord," Dam said as he kept driving toward his destination.

Epilogue

Saul stood in the outer court with legions of angels watching Don Shepherd make his entry through the pearly gates of heaven. Saul had fought many battles for the Shepherd family. He'd endured much to bring Dam Shepherd to the point of understanding his calling. He never imagined the kid would be a vessel used to get his grandfather to heaven. Saul nudged the angel next to him and pointed toward Don, the earthly king pin.

"Look at God. His wonders never cease," the angel said.

Don's eyes widened as he viewed the splendor of heaven. From greener than green grass to the most glorious flowers with vivid and brilliant colors that Don had ever seen. He was drawn to a flower bed on the other side of the cushiony cloud laden streets. The colors kept changing from bright red, to vivid white, to a glorious orange.

Don was mesmerized by everything that was going on around him. The music was like no music he'd ever heard, but it was also the most beautiful sound that his ears had ever experienced. As he stepped into the flower bed, another sound intrigued him and caused him to turn in the direction of the group that had gathered just outside the flowerbed. They were saying, "Glory to God in the highest. For He has done great things."

The group that had gathered had on white robes with crowns on their heads. Each person had numerous jewels on their crown. They bowed low, then got back up and repeated that phrase again. "Glory to God in the highest. For He has done great things."

"It gives us great joy to praise God in the Garden of Love."

Don heard the woman's voice behind him. It was a voice that he'd heard every day of his life until he was twelve years old. He swung around to come face to face with Starlight. She wore a radiant robe and had a crown on her head that held one radiant jewel.

Starlight pointed toward the group. "Do you see all the jewels in their crowns. Those jewels are for the souls they helped bring into heaven. Those men were mighty evangelist for the Lord when they were on earth."

Don pointed at the single jewel on Starlight's crown. "Why do you have that jewel?"

Starlight reached up and touched her crown. She smiled. "It must have just appeared. I didn't even know it was there." She reached out and wrapped her arms around Don and embraced him as she had longed to do while on earth. "I prayed for this moment with my last breath. God has been gracious to me, for He has delivered you to heaven so that I might hold you in my arms one more time."

With wonderment in his eyes, Don asked her, "Is that jewel for me, Mama?"

"Yes, my son. But I have it on good authority that your offspring will have too many jewels for a mere crown, they will be wearing coats with imbedded jewels when they arrive."

"You don't say," Don smiled as he and his mother walked through the flowerbed rejoicing at what the good Lord had done.

The end of Book V

Stay tuned for Book VI, Servant of God coming in August 2018

Don't forget to join my mailing list:

http://vanessamiller.com/events/join-mailing-list/

Join me on Facebook: https://www.facebook.com/groups/77899021863/

Join me on Twitter: https://www.twitter.com/vanessamiller01

Family Business Series

Family Business I

Family Business II - Sword of Division

Family Business III - Love and Honor

Family Business IV - The Children

Family Business V - Servant of God

About the Author

Vanessa Miller is a best-selling author, playwright, and motivational speaker. She started writing as a child, spending countless hours either reading or writing poetry, short stories, stage plays, and novels. Vanessa's creative endeavors took on new meaning in1994 when she became a Christian. Since then, her writing has been centered on themes of redemption, often focusing on characters facing multi-dimensional struggles.

Vanessa's novels have received rave reviews, with several appearing on *Essence Magazine's* Bestseller's List. Miller's work has receiving numerous awards, including "Best Christian Fiction Mahogany Award" and the "Red Rose Award for Excellence in Christian Fiction." Miller graduated from Capital University with a degree in Organizational Communication. She is an ordained minister in her church, explaining, "God has called me to minister to readers and to help them rediscover their place with the Lord."

She has worked with numerous publishers: Urban Christian, Kimani Romance, Abingdon Press and Whitaker House. She is currently Indy published through Praise Unlimited enterprises and working on the Family Business Series.

In 2016, Vanessa launched the Christian Book Lover's Retreat in an effort to bring readers and authors of Christian fiction together in an environment that's all about Faith, Fun & Fellowship. To learn more about Vanessa, please visit her website: www.vanessamiller.com. If you would like to know more about the Christian Book Lover's Retreat that is currently held in Charlotte, NC during the last week in October, you can visit: http://www.christianbookloversretreat.com/index.html

Don't forget to join my mailing list:
http://vanessamiller.com/events/join-mailing-list/
Join me on Facebook: https://www.facebook.com/groups/77899021863/
Join me on Twitter: https://www.twitter.com/vanessamiller01

CPSIA information can be obtained
at www.ICGtesting.com
Printed in the USA
LVHW051216260223
740443LV00009B/913

9 781984 169389